Never has Theodore Sturgeon been in more brilliant form than in this collection of short stories. From the problems of *How To Kill Aunty* (which isn't as easy as you might think!) to the enchanting language and devastating denouement of *The World Well Lost* he proves himself yet again a master of the science fiction genre. Established fans will hail this book as a further milestone in Sturgeon's career, while anyone who is new to his writing will have the delight of discovering an author who is guaranteed to become a firm favourite.

STARSHINE is a masterpiece – so read on.

Also by Theodore Sturgeon in Sphere Books:
VENUS PLUS X

Starshine

Theodore Sturgeon

SPHERE BOOKS LIMITED
30/32 Gray's Inn Road, London WC1X 8JL

First published in Great Britain
by Victor Gollancz Ltd 1968

Copyright © Theodore Sturgeon 1966

First Sphere Books edition 1978

For Louis Feinberg and his lovely Anne
in gratitude for their friendship and trust

TRADE MARK

Filmset in Photon Times

Printed in Great Britain by
C. Nicholls & Company Ltd
The Philips Park Press, Manchester

CONTENTS

'DERM FOOL'

I am not generally a fussy man. A bit of litter around my two-and-a-half-room dugout on the West Side seldom bothers me. What trash that isn't big enough to be pushed out in the hallway can be kicked around till it gets lost. But today was different. Myra was coming, and I couldn't have Myra see the place this way.

Not that she cared particularly. She knew me well enough by this time not to mind. But the particular *kind* of litter might be a bit – disturbing.

After I had swept the floor I began looking in odd corners. I didn't want any vagrant breeze to send unexplainable evidence fluttering out into the midst of the room – not while Myra was there. Thinking about her, I was almost tempted to leave one of the things where she could see it. She was generally so imperturbable – it might be amusing to see her hysterical.

I put the unchivalrous thought from me. Myra had always been very decent to me. I was a bit annoyed at her for making me like her so much when she was definitely not my type. Crawling under the bed, I found my slippers. My feet were still in them. I set one on top of the mantel and went into the other room, where I could sit down and wrench the foot out of the other slipper. They were odd slippers; the left was much bigger than the right. I swore and tugged at that right foot. It came out with a rustle; I rolled it up in a ball and tossed it into the waste-paper basket. Now let's see – oh, yes, there was a hand still clutching the handle of one of the bureau drawers. I went and pried it off. Why the deuce hadn't Myra called me up instead of wiring? No chance to head her off now. She'd just drift in, as usual. And me with all this on my mind –

I got the index finger off the piano and threw it and the left foot away, too. I wondered if I should get rid of the torso hanging in the hall closet, but decided against it. That was a fine piece. I might be able to make something good out of it; a suitcase, perhaps, or a rainproof sports jacket. Now that I had all this raw material, I might as well turn it to my advantage.

I checked carefully. My feet were gone, so I wouldn't have to worry about them until the morning. My right hand, too; that was good. It would be awful to shake hands with Myra and have her find herself clinging to a disembodied hand. I pulled at the left. It seemed a little loose, but I didn't want to force it. This wasn't a painful disease as long as you let it have its own way. My face would come off any minute now. I'd try not to laugh too much; maybe I could keep it on until she had gone.

I put both hands around my throat and squeezed a little. My neck popped and the skin sloughed dryly off. Now that was all right. If I wore a necktie, Myra wouldn't be able to see the crinkling edges of skin just above my collarbone.

The doorbell buzzed and I started violently. As I stood up, the skin of my calf parted and fell off like a cellophane gaiter. I snatched it up and stuffed it under a sofa pillow and ran for the door. As I reached it, one of my ears gave a warning crackle; I tore it off and put it in my pocket and swung the door wide.

'David!' She said that, and it meant that she was glad to see me, and that it had been eight months since the last time, and she was feeling fine, and she was sorry she hadn't written, but then she never wrote letters – not to anybody.

She swooped past me into the room, paused as if she were folding wings, shrugged out of her coat without looking to see if I were there behind her to take it, because she knew I was, crossed her long legs and

8

three-pointed gently on the rug. I put a cigarette into one extended hand and a kiss in the palm of the other, and it wasn't until then that she looked at me.

'Why – David! You're looking splendid! Come here. What have you done to your face? It's all crinkly. It looks sweet. You've been working too hard. Do I look nice? I feel nice. Look, new shoes. Snakeskin. Speaking of snakes, how are you, anyway?'

'Speaking of snakes, Myra, I'm going to pieces. Little pieces, that detach themselves from me and flutter in the gusts of my furious labouring. Something has got under my skin.'

'How awful,' she said, not really hearing me. She was looking at her nails, which were perfect. 'It isn't because of me, is it? Have you been pining away for me, David? David, you still can't marry me, in case you were going to ask.'

'I wasn't going to ask, but it's nice to know, anyway,' I said. My face fell, and I grabbed it and hid it under my coat. She hadn't seen, thank heavens! That meant I was relatively secure for a few hours. There remained only my left hand. If I could get rid of it – good heavens! It was already gone!

It might be on the doorknob. Oh, she mustn't see it! I went into the foyer and searched hurriedly. I couldn't find it anywhere. Suppose it had caught in her wraps? Suppose it were on the floor somewhere near where she was sitting? Now that I was faced with it, I knew I couldn't bear to see her hysterical. She was such a – a *happy* person to have around. For the millionth time since that skinning knife had slipped, I muttered, 'Now, why did this have to happen to *me*?'

I went back into the living room. Myra was still on the floor, though she had moved over under the light. She was toying curiously with the hand, and the smile on her face was something to see. I stood there speechless, waiting for the storm. I was used to it by this time, but Myra —

She looked up at me swiftly, in the birdlike way she had. She threw her glances so quickly that you never knew just how much she had seen — under all her chatter and her glittering idiosyncrasies was as calm and astute a brain as ever hid behind glamour.

The hand — it was not really a hand, but just the skin of one — was like a cellophane glove. Myra slipped it on her own and peeped through the fingers at me. 'Hiya, fellow reptile,' she giggled; and suddenly the giggles changed into frightened little squeaks, and she was holding out her arms to me, and her lovely face was distorted by tears so that it wasn't lovely any more, but sweet — oh, so darned sweet! She clung close to me and cried pitifully, 'David, what are we going to *do*?'

I held her tight and just didn't know what to say. She began talking brokenly: 'Did it bite you, too, David? It bit m-me, the little beast. The Indians worship it. Th-they say its bite will ch-change you into a snake. . . . I was afraid. . . . Next morning I began shedding my skin every twenty-four hours — and I have ever since.' She snuggled even closer, and her voice calmed a little. It was a lovely voice, even now. 'I could have killed the snake, but I didn't because I had never seen anything like it, and I thought you might like to have it — so I sent it, and now it's bitten you, and you're losing your skin all the time, too, and — oh-h-h!'

'Myra, don't. Please, don't. It didn't bite me. I was skinning it, and my knife slipped. I cut myself. The snake was dead when I got it. So — *you're* the one who sent it! I might have known. It came with no card or letter; of *course* it was you! How . . . how long have you been this way?'

'F-four months.' She sniffed, and blew her pink nose on my lapel because I had forgotten to put a hand-kerchief in my breast pocket. 'I didn't care after . . . after

10

I found out that it didn't hurt, and that I could count on when parts of my skin would come off. I – thought it would go away after a while. And then I saw your hand in a store window in Albuquerque. It was a belt buckle – a hand holding a stick, with the wrist fastened to one end of the belt and the stick to the other; and I bought it and saw what it was, because the hand was stuffed with the perfumed moulage you always use for your humming-bird brooches and things – and anyway, you were the only one who *could* have designed such a fascinating belt, or who *would* have thought to use your own skin just because . . . because you happened to have it around – and I hated myself then and I-loved you for it –' She twisted out of my arms and stared into my eyes, amazement written on her face, and joy. 'And I do love you for it, right *now*, David, *now*, and I never loved anyone else before and I don't care' – she plucked my other ear, and the skin rustled away in her hand – 'if you *are* all dilapidated!'

I saw it all now. Myra's crazy desire to climb a mesa, one of those island tableaux of the desert, where flora and fauna have gone their own ways these thousand thousand years; her discovering the snake, and catching it for me because I was a combination taxidermist and jeweller, and she had never seen anything like it and thought I might want it. Crazy, brave thing; she had been bitten and had said nothing to anybody because 'it didn't hurt'; and then, when she found out that I had the same trouble, she had come streaking to New York to tell me it was her fault!

'If you feel that way about it, Myra,' I said gently, 'then I don't care at all about this . . . this dry rot . . . little snake in the grass –' I kissed her.

Amazing stuff, this cast-off skin. Regularly as clockwork, every twenty-four hours, the epidermis would toughen, loosen and slip off. It was astonishingly

11

cohesive. My feet would leave their skin inside my slippers, keeping the exact shape of the limb on which it had grown. Flex the dead skin a couple of times, and it would wrinkle in a million places, become limp and flexible. The nails would come off, too, but only the top-most layer of cells. Treated with tannic acid and afterward with wool oil, it was strong, translucent and soft. It took shellac nicely, and a finish of Vandyke-brown oil paint mixed with bronze powder gave a beautiful old-gold effect. I didn't know whether I had an affliction or a commodity.

That snake — It was about four feet long, thicker at head and tail than it was in the middle. It was a lustreless orange, darker underneath than it was on top, but it was highly fluorescent. It smelled strongly of honey and formic acid, if you can imagine that for yourself. It had two fangs, but one was on top of its mouth and the other on the lower jaw. Its tongue was forked, but at the roots only; it had an epiglottis, seven sets of rudimentary limbs and no scales. I call it a snake because it was more nearly a snake than anything else. I think that's fair. Myra is mostly a Puckish angel, but you can still call her a woman. See? The snake was a little of this and a little of that, but I'll swear its origin was not of *this* earth. We stood there hand in hand, Myra and I, staring at the beast, and wondering what to do about it all.

'We might get rich by renting it to side shows,' said Myra.

'Nobody would believe it. How about renting ourselves to the A. M. A.?' I asked.

She wrinkled her nose and that was out. Tough on the A. M. A.

'What are we going to do about it, David?' She asked me as if she thought I knew and trusted me because of it, which is a trick that altogether too many women know.

'Why, we'll –' And just then came the heavy pounding on the door.

Now, there is only one animal stupid enough to bang on a door when there is a bell to ring, and that is a policeman. I told Myra to stay there in the lab and wait, so she followed me into the foyer.

'You David Worth?' asked the man. He was in plain clothes, and he had a very plain face.

'Come in,' I said.

He did, and sat down without being asked, eyeing the whisky decanter with little but evident hope. 'M'name's Brett. H. Brett.'

'H. for Halitosis?' asked Myra gently.

'Naw, Horace. What do I look like, a Greek? Hey, headquarters's checkin' on them ornaments o' y'rs, Mr. Worth.' The man had an astonishing ability to masticate his syllables. 'They look like they're made of human skin. Y'r a taxidoimist, ain'tcha?'

'I am. So?'

'So where'dja get th' ror material? Pleece analysis says it's human skin. What do you say?'

I exchanged a glance with Myra. 'It is,' I said.

It was evidently not the answer Brett expected. 'Ha!' he said triumphantly. 'Where'd you get it, then?'

'Grew it.'

Myra began to skip about the room because she was enjoying herself. Brett picked up his hat from the floor and clung to it as if it were the only thing he could trust. I began to take pity on him.

'What did they do down there, Brett? Microscopic cross-section? Acid and base analyses?'

'Yeah.'

'Tell me; what have they got down there – hands?'

'Yeah, and a pair o' feet. Book ends.'

'You always did have beautiful feet, darling,' caroled Myra.

'Tell you what I'll do, Brett,' I said. I got a sheet of

13

paper, poured some ink on to a blotter, and used it as a stamp pad. I carefully put each fingertip in the ink and pressed it to the paper. 'Take that down to headquarters and give it to your suspicious savants. Tell them to compare these prints with those from the ornaments. Write up your reports and turn them in with a recommendation that the whole business be forgotten; for if it isn't I shall most certainly sue the city, and you, and anyone else who gets in my way, for defamation of character. I wouldn't consider it impolite, Mr. Brett, if you got out of here right away, without saying good night.' I crossed the room and held the door open for him.

His eyes were slightly glazed. He rose and walked carefully around Myra, who was jumping up and down and clapping her hands, and scuttled out. Before I could close the door again he whirled and stuck his foot in it.

'Lissen. I don't know what's goin' on here, see? Don't you or that lady try to leave here, see? I'm havin' the place watched from now on, see? You'll hear from me soon's I get to headquarters, see?'

'You're a big seesee,' said Myra over my shoulder; and before I could stop her she plucked off her nose and threw it in the detective's face. He moved away, so fast that he left his hat hanging in mid-air; seconds later we heard the violence of his attempted passage down four flights of stairs when there were only three.

Myra danced three times around the room and wound up at the top of the piano – no mean feat, for it was a bulky old upright. She sat there laughing and busily peeling off the rest of her face.

'A certain something tells me,' I said when I could talk, which was after quite awhile, 'that you shouldn't have done that. But I'm glad you did. I don't think Detective Inspector Horace Halitosis Brett will be around any more.'

Myra gestured vaguely toward her bag. I tossed it to

14

her, and she began dabbing at nose and lips in the skilful, absent way women have. 'There,' she said when she had finished. 'Off with the old – on with the new.'

'You're the first woman in creation who gets beauty treatments in spite of herself. Pretty neat.'

'Not bad,' she said impersonally to her mirror. 'Not bad, Myra!'

Thinking of her, watching her, made me suddenly acutely conscious of her. It happens that way sometimes. You know you love the gal, and then suddenly you *realize* it. 'Myra –'

I think she had a gag coming, but when she looked at me she didn't say anything. She hopped down off the piano and came over to me. We stood there for a long time.

'You sleep in there,' I said, nodding toward the bedroom. 'I'll –'

She put her arms around me. 'David –'

'Mm-m-m?'

'I'll – have a nice torso for you at 12:48 –'

So we stuck around and talked until 12:48.

It must have been about two weeks later, after we were married, that she started breaking bottles in my laboratory. She came into the laboratory one afternoon and caught me cold. I was stirring a thick mass in a beaker and sniffing at it, and was so intent on my work that I never heard her come in. She moved like thistledown when she wanted to.

'What are you cooking, darling?' she asked as she put away a beautiful pair of arms she had just 'manufactured'.

I put the beaker on the bench and stood in front of it. 'Just some . . . sort of . . . er . . . stickum I'm mixing up for – Myra, beat it, will you? I'm busy as –'

She slid past me and picked up the beaker. 'Hm-m-m. Pretty. *Sniff*. Honey and – formic acid. Using the smell

15

of that beast as a lead, are you? Dr. David Worth, trying to find a cure for a gold mine. It's a cure, isn't it? Or trying to be?' Her tone was very sweet. Boy, was she sore!

'Well ... yes,' I admitted. I drew a deep breath. 'Myra, we can't go on like this. For myself I don't care, but to have you spending the rest of your life shedding your epidermis like a ... a blasted cork oak – it's too much. You've been swell about it, but I can't take it. You're too swell, and it's too much for my conscience. Every time I come in here and start stuffing something of yours, I begin worrying about you. It hasn't been bad, so far – but, woman, think of it! The rest of your life, sloughing off your hide, worrying about whether or not you can find somewhere to take your face off when you're not home; trying to remember where you dropped a hand or a leg. You – Myra, you're not listening.'

'Of course I'm not. I never listen to you when you're talking nonsense.'

'It isn't nonsense!' I was getting sore.

'I wonder,' she said dreamily, sloshing the mess around in the beaker, 'whether this thing will bounce.' She dropped it on the floor and looked curiously. It didn't bounce. I stood there fumbling for a cuss word strong enough, and wondering whether or not I could move fast enough to poke her one.

'David, listen to me. How long have you been a taxidermist?'

'Oh – eleven years. What's that got –'

'Never mind. And how much money have you saved in eleven years?'

'Well, none, until recently. But lately –'

'Quiet. And you have eight hundred-odd in the bank now. Those stuffed-skin gadgets sell faster than we can make them. And just because you have some funny idea that I don't like to give you my – by-products, you want

16

to cut the water off, go back to stuffing squirrels and humming birds for buttons. David, you're a fool — a derm fool.'

'That's not very punny.'

She winced. 'But here's the main thing, David. You've got this trouble, and so have I. We've been cashing in on it, and will, if only you'll stop being stupid about it. The thing I like about it is that we're partners — I'm *helping* you. I love you. Helping you means more to me than — Oh, David, can't you see? Can't you?'

I kissed her. 'And I thought you were just a good sport,' I whispered. 'And I thought some of it was mock heroics. Myra —' Oh, well. She won. I lost. Women are funny that way. But I still had an idea or two about a cure —

I'd been wrong about the indefatigable Inspector Brett. It was Myra who found out that he was tailing us everywhere, parking for hours in a doorway across the street, and sometimes listening at the door. I'd never have known it; but, as I've pointed out before, Myra has superhuman qualities. When she told me about it, I was inclined to shrug it off. He didn't have anything on us. I had to laugh every time I thought of what must have gone on at police headquarters when they checked up on my fingerprints and those of the hands they had bought in the stores.

The fact that it was human skin, and that the prints were identical in dozens of specimens, must have given them a nasty couple of days. Prove that the axiom about two points and a straight line is false, and where's your whole science of geometry? And prove that there can be not only identical fingerprints, but *dozens* of identical ones, and you have a lot of experts walking around in circles and talking to themselves.

Brett must have appointed himself to crack this case. I was quite willing to let him bang his head against a wall. It would feel nice when he stopped. I should have known Myra better. She had a glint in her eye when she talked about that gang buster.

In the meantime I kept working on that cure. I felt like a heel to skulk around behind Myra's back that way. You see, she trusted me. We'd had that one row about it, and I'd given in. That was enough for her. She wouldn't spy on me when I was working alone in the lab; and I knew that if she did realize it, suddenly, she would be deeply hurt. But this thing was too big. I *had* to do what I was doing, or go nuts.

I had a lead. The formic-honey idea was out, as a cure, though certain ingredients in them, I was sure, had something to do with the cause. That cause was amazingly simple. I could put it down here in three words. But do you think I would? *Heh.* I've got a corner on this market –

But this was my lead: My *hair* never came off! And I wear a miniscule moustache; every time my face came off it left the moustache. I have very little body hair; now, with this trouble, I had none. It came off, for the follicles were comparatively widely separated. First, I thought that this phenomenon was due to a purely physical anchorage of the skin by the hair roots. But, I reasoned, if that had been the case, layer after layer of skin would have formed under my moustache. But that did not happen. Evidently, then, this amazing separative and regenerative process was nullified by something at the hair roots. I could tell you what it was, too, but – I should knife myself in the back!

I worked like a one-armed pianist playing Mendelssohn's 'Spinning Song'. It took months, but by repeated catalysis and refinement, I finally had a test tube full of clear golden liquid. And – know what it was? Look: I hate to be repetitious, but I'm not saying. Let it suffice that it can be bought by the gallon at your corner drugstore. Nobody knew about it as a cure for my peculiar disease — if you want to call it that — because as far as I know no one had ever seen the disease before. *Bueno*.

Then I went to work on the cause. It didn't take long. As I have said, the most baffling thing about the trouble was its simplicity.

In the windup, I had it. An injection to cause the trouble, a lotion to cure or isolate it. I got ten gallons of each fluid — no trouble, once I knew what to get — and then began worrying about how to break the news to Myra.

'Kirro,' I said to her one day, 'I want a good face from you tonight. I want to make a life mask of you. Have to get all set first, though. You lose your face at 8:45, don't you? Well, come into the lab at 8:30. We'll plaster you with clay, let it dry so that it draws the face off evenly, back it with moulage, and wash the clay off after the moulage has hardened. Am I brilliant?'

'You scintillate,' she said. 'It's a date.'

I started mixing the clay, though I knew I wouldn't use it. Not to take her face off, anyway. I felt like a louse.

She came in on time as if she hadn't even looked at a clock — how I envy her that trick! — and sat down. I dipped a cloth in my lotion and swabbed her well with it. It dried immediately, penetrating deeply. She sniffed.

'What's that?'

'Sizing,' I said glibly.

'Oh. Smells like —'

'*Shh.* Someone might be listening.' That for you, dear reader!

I went behind her with a short length of clothesline. She lay back in the chair with her eyes closed, looking very lovely. I leaned over and kissed her on the lips, drawing her hands behind her. Then I moved fast. There was a noose at each end of the line; I whipped one around her wrists, drew it tight, threw it under the back

19

rung of the chair, and dropped the other end over her head. 'Don't move, darling,' I whispered. 'You'll be all right if you keep still. Thrash around and you'll throttle yourself.' I put the clock where she could see it and went out of there. I don't want to hear my very best beloved using that kind of language.

She quieted down after about ten minutes. 'David!'

I tried not to listen.

'David – please!'

I came to the door. 'Oh, David, I don't know what you're up to, but I guess it's all right. Please come here where I can look at you. I . . . I'm afraid!'

I should have known better. Myra was never afraid of anything in her life. I walked over and stood in front of her. She smiled at me. I came closer. She kicked me in the stomach. 'That's for tying me up, you . . . you heel. Now, what goes on?'

After I got up off the floor and got my gasping done, I said, 'What time is it, bl – er, light of my life?'

'Ten minutes to ni – David! David, what have you done? Oh, you fool! You utter dope! I told you – Oh, *David!*' And for the second and last time in my life, I saw her cry. Ten minutes to nine and her face was still on. Cured! – at least, her face. I went behind her where she couldn't reach me.

'Myra, I'm sorry I had to do it this way. But – well, I know how you felt about a cure. I'd never have been able to talk you into taking it. This was the only way. What do you think of me now, stubborn creature?'

'I think you're a pig. Terribly clever, but still a pig. Untie me. I want to make an exit.'

I grinned. 'Oh, no. Not until the second-act curtain. Don't go away!' I went over to the bench and got my hypodermic. 'Don't move, now. I don't want to break this mosquito needle off in your jaw.' I swabbed her gently around the sides of the face with the lotion, to localize the shot.

20

'I . . . hope your intentions are honourable,' she said through clenched teeth as the needle sank into the soft flesh under her jawbone. 'I – Oh! Oh! It . . . itches. David –'

Her face went suddenly crinkly. I caught her skin at the forehead and gently peeled it off. She stared wide-eyed, then said softly:

'I can't kiss you, marvellous man, unless you untie me –'

So I did, and she did, and we went into the living room where Myra could rejoice without breaking anything of value.

In the middle of a nip-up she stopped dead, brainwave written all over her face. 'David, we're going to do some entertaining.' She sat there in the middle of the floor and began to scream. And I mean she could scream.

In thirty seconds flat, heavy footsteps – also flat – pounded on the stairs, and Brett's voice bellowed: 'Op'n up in th' name o' th' law!' He's the only man I ever met who could mumble at the top of his voice.

Myra got up and ran to the door. 'Oh – Mr. Brett. How nice,' she said in her best hostess voice. 'Do come in.'

He glowered at her. 'What's goin' *on* here?'

She looked at him innocently. 'Why, Mr. Brett –'

'Was you screamin'?'

She nodded brightly. 'I like to scream. Don't you?'

'Naw. What'a idear?'

'Oh, sit down and I'll tell you about it. Here. Have a drink.' She poured him a tumbler of whisky so strong I could almost see it raise its dukes. She pushed him into a chair and handed it to him. 'Drink up. I've missed you.'

He goggled up at her uncertainly. 'Well – I dunno. Gee, t'anks. Here's how, Miz Worth.' And he threw it down the hatch. It was good stuff. Each of his eyes independently scanned his nose. He blinked twice and regretfully set the glass down. She refilled it, signalling behind her back for me to shut up. I did. When Myra acts this way there is nothing to do but stand by and wonder what's going to happen next.

Well, she got Brett started on the history of his life. Every two hundred words he'd empty that glass. Then she started mixing them. I was afraid that would happen. Her pet — for others' consumption; she wouldn't touch it — was what she called a 'Three-two-one'. Three fingers of whisky, two of gin, one of soda. Only in Brett's case she substituted rum for the soda. Poor fellow.

In just an hour and a half he spread out his arms, said, 'Mammy!' and folded up.

Myra looked down at him and shook her head. '*Tsk, tsk.* Pity I didn't have any knockout drops.'

'Now what?' I breathed.

'Get your hypo. We're going to infect John Law here.'

'Now, Myra — wait a minute. We can't —'

'Who says? Come on, David — he won't know a thing. Look — here's what we'll do with him.'

She told me. It was a beautiful idea. I got my mosquito, and we went to work. We gave him a good case; shots of the stuff all over his body. He slept peacefully through it all, even the gales of merriment. The more we thought of it — Ah, poor fellow!

After we had what we wanted from him I undressed him and swabbed him down with the lotion. He'd be good as new when he came to. I put him to bed in the living room, and Myra and I spent the rest of the night working in the lab.

When we finished, we took the thing and set it in the living room. Brett's breathing was no longer stertorous; he was a very strong man. Myra tiptoed in and put the alarm clock beside him. Then we watched from the crack of the laboratory door.

The first rays of the sun were streaming through the windows, lighting up our masterpiece. The alarm went off explosively; Brett started, groaned, clutched his head. He felt around for the clock, knocked it off the chair. It fell shouting under the daybed. Brett groaned again, blinked his eyes open. He stared at the window first, trying vaguely to find out what was wrong with it. I could almost hear him thinking that, somehow, he didn't know where he was. The clock petered out. Brett began to stare dazedly about the room. The ceiling, the walls, and —

There in the geometric centre of the room stood Detective Inspector Horace Brett, fully clothed. His shield glittered in the sun. On his face was a murderous leer, and in his hand was a regulation police hogleg, trained right between the eyes of the man on the bed. They stared at each other for ten long seconds. The man with the hangover and the man's skin with the gun. Then Brett moved.

Like a streak of light he hurtled past the effigy. My best corduroy bedspread streaming behind him, clad only in underwear and a wrist watch, he shot through the door — and I mean *through*, because he didn't stop to open it — and wavered shrieking down the stairs. I'd never have caught him if he hadn't forgotten again that there were only three flights of stairs there. He brought up sharp against the wall; I was right behind him. I caught him up and toted him back up to the apartment before the neighbours had a chance to come rubbering around. Myra was rolling around on the floor. As I came in with Brett, she jumped up and kissed his gun-toting image, calling it fondly a name that should have been reserved for me.

We coddled poor Brett and soothed him; healed his wounds and sobered him up. He was sore at first and then grateful; and, to give him due credit, he was a good sport. We explained everything. We didn't have to

23

swear him to secrecy. We had the goods on him. If I hadn't caught up with him, he'd have run all the way to headquarters in his snuggies.

It was not an affliction, then; it was a commodity. The business spread astonishingly. We didn't let it get too big; but what with a little false front and a bit more ballyhoo, we are really going places. For instance, in Myra's exclusive beauty shop is a booth reserved for the wealthiest patrons. Myra will use creams and lotions galore on her customer by way of getting her into the mood; then, after isolating the skin on her face, will infect it with a small needle. In a few minutes the skin comes off; a mud pack hides it. The lady has a lovely smooth new face; Myra ships the old one over to my place where my experts mount it. Then, through Myra's ballyhoo, the old lady generally will come around wanting a life mask. I give her a couple of appointments – they amount to séances – sling a lot of hocus-pocus, and in due time deliver the mask – life-size, neatly tinted. They never know, poor old dears, that they have contracted and been cured of the damnedest thing that ever skipped inclusion in *Materia Medica*. It's a big business now; we're coining money.

Like all big business, of course, it has its little graft. A certain detective comes around three times a week for a thirty-second shave, free of charge. He's good people. His effigy still menaces our living room, with a toy gun now. Poor fellow.

THE HAUNT

Just a gag, that's all — a gag. I'm sure it was. It had to be. Heck, we were wise, Tommy and me. Tommy was a radio technician and a good one, and I knew the gadgets to the last hidden loud-speaker and the last Fahnestock clip almost as well as he did. Tommy was a funny egg, anyway. Foggy, you know — the kind of guy that shows up at work with one brown shoe and one black, or dunks his cafeteria check in his coffee and hands a doughnut to the waiter to punch. But — he knew his stuff, he had the apparatus, and the idea tickled him. I can see his point there. Scaring the living daylights out of a cool cookie like Miriam Jensen was a challenge to any man.

Her rock-hard nerves were by no means her only striking characteristic. She was smooth — smooth to look at, smooth to talk to, smooth in the way she thought and acted and moved. Tall, you know — dark brunette, long slim neck, small head and features; quite tall — that kind. A knockout. Brains, too, and she used them. I don't believe anything but hard exercise could raise her pulse more than one-two beats a minute. I know that the funny idea I had that it would be nice to be married to her didn't have her at all fluttery. She laughed me off. When I asked for her lily-white hand, did she say she'd be a sister to me? Did she tell me tenderly that we weren't suited? Did she say so much as 'No?' Uh-huh. She said: 'You're cute, Bill. Didn't anyone ever tell you how cute you were?' And she giggled. I stood there with my teeth in my mouth and my bare face hanging out, watching her walk away; and then and there I said to myself, 'I'm going to shake her off her high horse, by all that's unholy, if I have to kill her to do it.'

I came home – lived in an apartment hotel then – and met Tommy in the hall. I dragged him into my place, stuck a drink in his hand, and figuratively wept on his shoulder about it for the best part of an hour, while he sat there doddering his untidy hair up and down and watching the bubbles collect on the bottom of an ice cube.

'W-what do y-you want to do about it?' he asked.

'I told you – slap her down. If I could think of a way to slap her down so that it would do *me* some good, I'd do it, too. But you can't walk up to a woman, take a poke at her, and expect her to marry you for it.'

'You can with s-some women,' Tommy observed with the profundity of a confirmed celibate.

'Not with this one,' I snorted. 'No, I've got to scare the bustle cover off her, and then rescue her, maybe. Or show her that I'm not scared by the same thing. Or both. Got any ideas?'

'I th-think you're a ph-phoney, Bill.'

'I didn't mean your ideas about me. Come on – you're supposed to run to brains. Forget the personalities and let's have a brain wave or two.'

Tommy stared at the ceiling and gravely ground out his cigarette two inches away from an ash-tray. 'What's she sc-sc-frightened of, do you think?'

I walked up and down for a couple of minutes, trying to frown out an answer to that one. 'Nothing, as far as I've ever heard,' I said. 'Miriam will dive off a sixty-foot platform, or break a bronc, or drive a midget racer, and breathe no harder for it than she does after a fast conga. I tell you, that girl's nerves – if she has any – are made of iridium-plated piano wire.'

'I bet she's superstitious,' said Tommy.

'What? Ghosts, you mean? Huh. Could be, but what –'

'Easy.' Tommy set his half-empty glass down on the

floor from about waist height. 'We'll make her some ghosts – you'll rescue her from them.'

'Swell. What do we do – draw some magic squares on the hotel carpet around a pot of devil's brew or something?'

'N-no. We take a couple of coils of wire and my little public-speaking s-system, and maybe a few coloured lights and stuff. And we haunt a house. Th-then you bring your iridium girl friend in. J-just leave it to me.'

'That sounds like quite something, Tommy,' I said. I was so tickled with the idea that I remembered I hadn't had a drink and began pouring myself one. 'Miriam's a sucker for a dare. But the Lord help me if she ever found out about this.'

Tommy looked at me vaguely and grinned. 'I don't know nothin', ch-chief,' he said, and got up to go. 'I'll l-let you know what I dream up on this, B-Bill. Night.' He went through the door.

I thanked him, pulled him out of the bathroom, and saw him to the right door. I never did meet such a foggy fellow.

Inside of a week he had it rigged up and took me out there to look it over. The house was a chalet over a century old. It had hedges in front of it gone hog wild, and the once-green paint was a filthy grey. It had eleven-foot ceilings and Venetian shutters which were in the last stages of decay, full of tartar and cavities, as it were. I don't know how Tommy had got hold of it, but he had, and man, how he'd rigged it up!

'You s-see,' he explained, 'the old place has a history, too. There have been four murders here, and th-three suicides. The l-last guy who owned it starved to death in the cellar.' He motioned me after him and started through the weeds toward the back. I looked up at the gloomy old pile and shuddered. 'What are we going around the back for?' I asked.

'So the dust in the f-front hallway will look as if no one has been here in the last twenty years,' he said, opening a cellar window. 'G-go on – climb in.'

I did, and he tumbled in after me. He threaded his way through large piles of rubbish until he came to a partition. He opened a door in it and we found ourselves inside a neatly arranged control room. Pointing, Tommy said, 'See th-that board? There's a photo cell and relay laid across every door in the house. Any time anyone goes into a room I know which one it is by the number underneath the light. There's my mike over there, and a phonograph pick-up. There's a hot-air system in the house; I put the speaker in the furnace, and when I play my little collection of m-moans and groans and shrieks from those recordings, you c-can hear them all over the house. It sounds swell.'

'It does,' I grinned. 'But why do you have to know which room we're going to be in?'

'For the l-lights,' he said. He showed me a battery of half a dozen knife switches and a rheostat. 'Some of the lights are ultraviolet, and they shine on fluorescent paint on the opposite wall. You s-see something there, and when you turn your flashlight on it, it's gone. Some of the lights are photo flashes. Oh, it'll be quite a sh-show.'

'It sure will,' I said, delighted.

'Now, when you b-bring your little lump of dry ice in,' said Tommy – I gathered he was referring to Miriam – 'take her in the front way. Here – I've typed out all the stories about the p-people who died in this place, and all the dope about how and where they g-got knocked off. Tell her all the yarns and take her into all the rooms. You'll know what to expect. That's all I can do – you'll have to figure out the rest yourself.'

'You've done enough,' I said, slapping him on the back so that his glasses fell off and broke. He pulled another pair out of his pocket and put them on. 'Don't worry,' I said. 'This ought to cut some of her ice.'

He gave me a few more details and took me on a tour of the place. Then I took my typewritten sheets and went home to bone up on them. It should be a snap, I thought. Anyhow, it should have been.

I cornered Miriam two nights later. I came up behind her and whispered in her ear, 'Will you marry me?'

She said, 'Oh, hello, Bill,' without even turning around.

'Miriam,' I said hoarsely, 'I asked you a question!'

She gently slid her shoulder out from under my hand. 'And I said "Hello, Bill".' She grinned.

I gnashed my teeth and tried to be calm.

'Do you like ghosts?' I asked irrelevantly.

'Dunno. I never met one,' she said. 'Don't you ever ask girls to dance?'

'No,' I said. 'I sweep 'em off their feet on to the floor when I feel like dancing, which I don't right now. I want to talk about ghosts.'

'A safe subject,' she observed. I nodded my head toward one of those pieces of furniture euphemistically called love seats, and we threaded our way through the crowd of people — it was one of those parties that Reggie Johns used to throw for people he didn't know. That is, he'd invite six couples he knew and forty or fifty would arrive.

'In 1853,' I said oratorically, 'Joachin Grandt — spelled with a "d" — was murdered by person or persons unknown in the first floor back of an old Swiss chalet up in Grove Street. A rumour circulated to the effect that the room was haunted. This so depreciated the value of the house and grounds that Joachim's great-nephew, Harrison Grandt — also spelled with a "d" — tried to prove that it was not haunted by spending a night there. He was found the next morning by one Harry Fortunato, strangled to death in exactly the manner used by the aforementioned person or persons. Fortunato was so exercised by this strange turn of events that he rushed out of the house and broke his neck on the front steps.'

'All this is quite bewildering,' said Miriam softly, 'but it seems to me that it is hardly the thing to whisper into my shell-like ear when we could be dancing.'

'Damn it, Miriam –'

'– also spelled with a "d",' she interjected.

'Let me finish telling you about this. After Fortunato's death there were two more murders and two supposed suicides, all of them either stranglings or neck-breakings. Now, the house is supposed to be really haunted. They say you can really see the spooks and hear voices and rattles and so forth – all the fixin's. I found out where the place is.'

'Oh? And what might that have to do with –'

'You? Well, I've heard tell that you aren't afraid of man, woman or beast. I just wondered about ghosts.'

'Don't be childish, Bill. Ghosts live inside the heads of foolish people and pop out when the foolish people want to be frightened.'

'Not these ghosts.'

She regarded me amusedly. 'Don't tell me you've seen them?'

I nodded.

She said, 'That proves my point. Let's dance.'

She half rose, but I caught her wrist and yanked her back. I don't think she liked it. 'Don't tell me you're afraid to go and see for yourself, Iron Woman?'

'Nobody suggested it.'

'I just did.'

She stopped yearning toward the dance floor and settled back. 'Ah – so that's the idea. Go on – let's have it,' she said in a I-won't-do-it-but-I'd-like-to-hear-about-it tone of voice.

'We just go out there and investigate it,' I said. 'Frankly, I'd like to see your hair curl.'

30

'Let me get this straight,' she said. 'You and I are going out at this time of night to a deserted house in a deserted neighbourhood to catch us a ghost. Right?' Her raised eyebrow added, 'Monkey business, hey?'

'No!' I said immediately. 'No monkey business. My word on that.' Of course, Tommy's electrical ghosts were monkey business, but that was not what she and her eyebrow meant by monkey business.

'Real ghosts,' she mused. 'Bill, if this is some kind of a joke —'

'With me, lady,' I said with real sincerity, 'this is no joke.'

She insinuated herself out of the love seat on to her feet and said, 'Stand by, then, while I tell Reggie we're leaving. I came with Roger Sykes, but he doesn't have to know anything about it.'

While she was gone I got some grinning done. Just like clockwork, it was — this was the night Tommy had said he'd pick to throw a scare into her. She'd fallen for the bait better than I ever could have hoped, and it certainly looked as if everything was breaking my way. Maybe if I could get her scared enough we could head for Gretna Green. Could be — could be.

I saw her at the door, waiting for me. She was dressed in something skintight and yet flowing, with a long white panel front and back, and black shoulders and sides — I dunno — I'm no dressmaker, but the dress was like the rest of her — smooth. And now she had slipped a great black cloak over her shoulders that fell away from her body at the sides and looked like wings. What a woman! I sighed, envying myself because I was going to have her to myself for a few hours.

We climbed into my ancient but efficient old struggle buggy. 'Where is this place?' Miriam asked as I pulled away from the kerb.

I glanced at her, taking in the way she wound her cloak about her and writhed deeper into it. Every move

31

a miracle, I thought. 'I told you,' I said, keeping my thoughts to myself. 'Up on Grove Street, on top of Toad Hill, across the street from a junk yard.'

'I know about where it is,' she said. 'Tarry not, my fran' – pile some coal on and let's get there. I've always wanted to meet up with a ghost.'

Her tone was one I'd heard before, once in a while. The time, for instance, that one of the boys had been trying to lasso a post with a length of clothesline and she had grabbed it from him impatiently, saying, 'Dammit, Joe, you make me nervous. Here,' and had whirled it once and snagged the post on the first cast. And that other time when one of the horses from the riding academy broke its leg taking a hedge. While half a dozen people looked on, she picked up an edged stone and with one clean blow killed the horse. 'It was the only thing to do,' she explained bluntly. 'None of you blockheads have even started back to the academy for a gun yet. What do you want to do – leave the animal to lie here screaming for a solid hour?'

'What makes you that way?' I asked her. She looked at me questioningly. 'I mean, why are you always ducking in to do more or less violent things? Why don't you learn to knit?'

'I can knit,' she said shortly, in a voice that said, 'Oh, dry up.'

So I dried up, contenting myself with the joyful play of street lights on her darkened profile, and wondering if I were a heel to pull this sort of a trick. We drew up eventually in front of the house. Miriam got out and stared up at it. It loomed grey and forbidding in the light of a half-moon. Before it, striving their dark utmost to hide the front walk, were the tangled, twelve-foot hedges. The whole place had a greedily unkempt look – it was a dirty old panhandler of a house, begging the right to exist another moment. Miriam walked up to the hedge and stopped, and I don't know whether she was hesitating or just waiting for me. We went up the path together.

I noticed with satisfaction that Tommy had either taken a taxi or parked his car on another street. That had bothered me a little – he was damn clever, but a little short on foresight. When we reached the top of the steps I covertly touched the doorbell. There was no sound – it would light a bulb on Tommy's board so he'd know we were in. I handed Miriam one of the two flashlights I had stowed in the car and pushed open the door.

Miriam caught my arm. 'Ladies first, you clod,' she laughed, and slid in ahead of me.

The floor of the foyer settled two inches under her feet with a bump; she flailed one arm a little to get her balance and turned to me, smiling coolly. 'Coming, Bill?'

We found ourselves in a high, narrow hallway containing a flight of stairs far too big for it.

'*Hello-o-o! Who's the-e-e-ere –*'

'Huh?' Miriam and I asked each other. The voice had been tiny, just the echo of an echo, but clear as a bos'n's pipe. 'I didn't say anything,' we chorused, and then Miriam said, 'Either we're not the only investigators or the ghosts are wasting no time on us. Either way, I like it here. Where to first, Bill?'

She'll have to get a little more scared than that before I can show her up, I thought. 'Upstairs,' I said. 'We'll start at the top and work down.'

Side by side, we headed up the old steps, scything great lumps of darkness away with our lights. At the first landing, Miriam walked ahead, as the stairs narrowed here. As she crossed the landing, I saw her heel sink as her weight whipped a loose board up on end. I caught it just before it could belt the back of her head.

'Thanks, pal,' she said evenly. 'I'll do the same for you some time.' Never turned a hair!

33

Almost at the top, I thought I heard something. 'Don't look now,' I said in a hushed voice, 'but I don't want you to miss anything, and I think I hear someone laughing.'

We froze and stopped breathing to give the faint sound a chance. 'That isn't laughing,' said Miriam.

I listened more carefully. 'Check,' I said, 'but from the sound of it, whatever is being laughed about should be cried over. Good heavens, what a crazy sound.'

It was a burbly noise, so quiet it was almost intimate, and it sobbed in peals. Miriam snorted as if she were trying to blow an evil smell out of her nostrils. I wiped sweat off the palms of my hands. Where the hell had Tommy picked up *that* recording?

We tiptoed across the second-floor hall and Miriam pushed open a door. Dust swirled up as it swung noiselessly back, far faster than was warranted, and a great dim shape loomed up out of it.

Smash!

A splintering crash behind us, and that unimaginable something ahead of us. I jumped to the right and Miriam to the left, and for a second the whole world was made of flailing electric beams and hidden menace. Miriam, to be frank, calmed down first; at least, enough to steady her flashlight on one of the sources of our panic. It was the old print that had been hanging in the hallway. Its nail had pulled out of the loose plaster, probably because of one of my dainty No. 10 footfalls, and it had fallen to the floor, smashing the glass in the picture frame. I shot my light at the open door. Just inside was a tall piece of furniture, an old-fashioned secretary desk, covered with a dusty white cloth.

'A little jumpy, aren't you, Bill?' called Miriam cheerfully as she came over to me.

I thrust my tongue between my teeth so they wouldn't chatter so loudly, and tried to grin doing it. In that crazy light I think I got away with it. Miriam must have thought I felt fine, because she rather readily let me lead the way into the room.

There was nothing much there but dust and a couple of broken chairs. At the back of the room was another door. With Miriam treading on my heels, I went through it. I stood just inside, fencing with the blackness with my torch and seeing nothing, stepped aside to let Miriam in. Something touched me lightly on the shoulder –

Bong! Whee-hoo! Bong! Whee-hoo! Bong!

Miriam said 'Gha!' with an intake of breath and grabbed at my arm, making me drop my light. It thumped to the floor and went out, and she pawed at hers, accidentally flipped the switch. Darkness hit us so hard our knees sagged under the weight of it, and my cold-blooded darling wrapped both arms around my head, which was the first thing she contacted; and she began making a noise like a duckling at the ripe old age of two hours. The bonging and whee-hooing went right on, until Miriam's hand, in a convulsive contraction, turned on her light again. We found ourselves staring up at an old-style cuckoo clock. It and its cuckoo were telling us the falsehood that it was eleven o'clock. I must have bumped into the pendulum and set it off.

Miriam stood there with her arms around me until the silly wooden bird had finished and retired; and yet a moment longer. This was my moment, and by damn if I wasn't too upset to appreciate it. Then she let me go, and said through a funny little smile, 'Bill – I think maybe this is comic. Laugh a bit, huh?'

I licked some moisture off my upper lip on to a dry tongue. 'Ha, ha,' I said without enthusiasm.

Miriam said firmly, 'The laughing noise was water in a pipe somewhere. That crash was a picture falling off the wall. We both saw it. The ... ah ... thing in the doorway was an old bookcase covered with a dust cloth. This last ghost of yours was a cuckoo clock. Right?'

35

'Right.'

'And that "Who's there" we heard when we came in was ... was — What was it, anyway?'

'Imagination,' I said promptly. 'Although I know damn well *I* didn't imagine it.'

'I did, then,' she said stubbornly, and added, 'Enough for both of us.' Her wry grin was a sight to behold.

'Must be,' I said, picking up my flashlight and trying to make my fingers behave enough to unscrew the reflector and slip in a spare bulb. I managed it, somehow. 'And are you by any slim chance imagining — *that*, too?' I pointed. She pivoted.

'That' was a blob of light on the wall, so dim it was all but invisible. The beam from her torch had been on another wall, or I wouldn't have seen it at all. As I stared breathlessly, looking at its shades and shadowy outlines, I began to make out what it was.

'It looks like a ... a neck!' whispered Miriam backing on to my feet. The thing was indeed a neck, flesh-pink and mottled with deep fingerlike gouges of blue-black. It held for just a few seconds and then faded out.

I gulped and said, 'Pretty!'

Miriam whipped her light around and splashed it on the wall. The beam wasn't steady, and she didn't say anything.

'Miriam — I feel like dancing, I think.'

'There's no music here,' she said quietly. 'We'd have to go somewhere else.'

'Yeah,' I said, and gulped. 'We would, wouldn't we?' But neither of us moved.

Finally she shrugged and took a deep breath. 'What are you waiting for, Bill? Let's go!'

'Go? Dancing, you mean?'

'Dancing!' she contraltoed scornfully. 'We were going to explore this house, weren't we? Come on, then.'

'Quite a feller, aren't you?' I said to her under my

36

breath. I think she heard me, because she squared her shoulders and went out. I tagged along.

It occurred to me that it was all very well to put on this show for her, but I was damned lucky that I'd picked her to pull it on rather than some more impressionable female. The place was getting under my skin as it was. Suppose I'd been with some twist who fainted or got hysterical or lost or something? Suppose I got left alone in this place? I began stepping on Miriam's heels.

We gave the rest of the second floor the once-over and nothing much happened. That pep talk of hers helped a lot. We casually dismissed sundry creaks and groans and rattlings as the wind in the chimneys, banging shutters, and settling floors. Neither of us saw fit to mention that there was no wind that night, and that a one-hundred-and-twenty-five-year-old house does not settle. In other words, we thought that nothing was bothering us at all until that sob-laughing started up again. That was pretty awful. Miriam had been holding hands with me for ten minutes before I realized it, and I only knew it at all when I felt her bones grate together as I clutched her when the laughing started. It ran up and down a whole tone scale, sounding like a palsied madman playing on a piano full of tears.

'Still like it here?' I asked.

'I didn't like school,' she said, 'but I graduated.'

We had to open a door to get on the stairs leading to the third floor. They were narrow with a turn in the middle, with a tiny square landing at the turn. I was in the lead – must have been a mistake, because you can bet I didn't ask for it, chivalry or no chivalry. Just before I reached the landing I saw a woman, a beautiful thing in diaphanous robes, walk gravely out of the wall at my right, across the landing and into the wall at my left. The only thing that detracted from her loveliness was the blood which spouted from her ears, and the fact

37

that I could see the patchy wall through her quite easily. I gasped and stepped back on Miriam's instep.

'Oo-o! Dammit, Bill –' She stood on her uninjured foot and clutched at the banister, a section of which immediately broke loose and went crashing and somersaulting into the darkness below.

'You all right?' I said over the reverberations.

I clutched at her to keep her from falling and managed only to get my thumb into her eye. She said something that her mother didn't teach her. 'Get away, Bill – you're a menace! What in the name of corruption did you step backward for?'

'Didn't you see her – it?' I said before I had sense enough to say nothing. She shook her head.

'Who?'

'A girl! She – Oh, skip it, Miriam. I guess I imagined that, too. Come on.'

We started to climb again, and something possessed us both to look back. At any rate, when I looked, it was over Miriam's head, and she was staring at the transparent woman, who was crossing back again from wall to wall across the landing. This time she walked backward, and the blood ran into her ears. It was infinitely more horrible than the first time, and yet, after the first shock of it I was comforted. For the first time Tommy had laid it on too thick. That reversed action was too cinematic to get over, I thought. And that's what it must have been – a film projected somewhere, perhaps out from under one of the steps, run forward and then backward. That would easily account for the transparency of the girl's figure, since it was projected directly against the wall. But – damn it, how did he ever achieve that astonishing three-dimensional effect?

'That,' Miriam was saying brokenly, 'is something that I just am not going to believe! Bill – for Heaven's sake, what sort of place is this?'

'Regular haunt, isn't it?' I said cheerfully. I was

feeling better now that I'd figured out one of the ghosts really to my satisfaction. 'Come on – we'll make our round and get out of here. The sooner the quicker, y'know!'

Her gait and her carriage and her expression, all I could catch in the sweeping beams of our torches, were almost meek. I suddenly felt overwhelmingly like a heel. This was a lousy thing to do to such a swell girl.

'Miriam,' I said softly, catching her arms, 'I –'

But just then the laughter reached a cold crescendo, and from downstairs came the most blood-freezing, ululating scream that it's ever been my sorrow to hear. It was the kind of sound to clamp a man's jaws so tight in terror that his gums bleed, and his skin goose-fleshes out like a woodrasp. The scream seemed to stop the laughter, for the stillness after it devoted itself to the scream's echoes; and we stopped breathing so that the sound of our breath would not keep the echoes alive. That scream didn't belong on this earth. Somewhere in hell is a damned soul which has been there long enough to be miserable enough and still stay strong enough to scream like that.

We pushed away from each other merely because it was the only movement we could make to thrust the remembrance of that sound from us a little. The desire to complete our tour of the chalet was something fevered and senseless and quite irresistible by now. We hurried to get it done – we made no slightest move to leave it partly finished. I couldn't have done it without my knowledge that no matter how extreme these horrors became, they were but the creations of Tommy's strange genius for handling electrical circuits. Miriam had her own iron nerve and the fact that so far I hadn't broken into a hysterical retreat.

The third floor wasn't bad – there was nothing there but odds and ends of old furniture, dust, and creaking floorboards. When we started downstairs we knew we were all but on our way out, and we grew almost cheerful. Almost. Not quite, because that noise began again – that creeping, tear-filled laughter. It went on and on and on, until we couldn't stand it any more, and it passed that point and still went on. We walked down steps and trotted down corridors and broke and ran in and out of rooms, playing childishly at being casual, while the laughter grew, not louder, but more and more clear; and we couldn't tell whether it was following us or whether it was simply everywhere. It was so all-enveloping that we lost consciousness of the fact that it was in the house. It was all around us, more than a sound – it was something we breathed, something which pressed our clothing to our shrinking bodies with its pulsings. It filled the whole world and there would never, never be an end to it, and we couldn't escape it by fleeing the house. We couldn't ever get away from it. It was part of us now, in our blood, in our bones. Rounding a corner on the first floor, Miriam crashed into a door and reeled back into my arms. I turned my light on her face. Part of the sound – some of it, all of it, I don't know – *was coming from her*!

'Miriam!' I screamed, and slapped her face twice, and clamped my hand over her writhing mouth. The laughter receded into the upper part of the house, and she sank tremblingly closer to me. 'Miriam – Why did I – Darling, come out of it. Listen to me! Mir –'

'Oh, Bill! Bill, I'm scared! I'm scared, Bill!' She said it quietly, in a small, very surprised voice; and then she began to cry, and I'll bet my eyeballs that it was the first time in her life she'd cried, because those tears came hard.

I picked her up in my arms and carried her into a room we hadn't yet visited. There was a monstrous old red plush and mahogany divan there, and I put her down on it. She put her arms around my neck and all of a sudden was a very little girl afraid of the dark. I

40

bent over her, all choked up, and for all I know, I cried, too.

The laughter approached again.

'Bill!' she wailed. 'Make it stop! Oh, please, please, make it stop!'

I couldn't keep up that pretence any longer. 'Stick around, bud,' I gritted; and, jamming one of the torches in an angle of the divan's rococo, I headed for the door.

Miriam sat up and screamed for me. I went back, put my arms around her and kissed her. She was so surprised when I let her go that she just sat there with her hand to her mouth, wordless, while I tore out and along the corridor to the steps that led down into the cellar.

Tommy's carried this thing too damn far, I gritted to myself as I cut into the littered cellar room where he had hidden his controls. There was such a thing as doing a job too well, and I was about to tell a radio engineer that, complete with fireworks. I fumbled along the wooden partition until I found the knothole he had used for a doorknob. I jammed a finger into it, whipped the door open, stabbed a ray of light inside. There wasn't anyone there. There just wasn't anyone in there at all!

'Tommy?' I sagged up against the partition, gasping. 'Tommy!' Nobody in there. No one working those lights, that switchboard, phonograph, no – 'Tommy!' I quavered.

The laughter kept on. On and on. I looked at the phonograph. It was there, all right, with its crystal pick-up and the wires running to the speaker in the old furnace. But it wasn't operating. I crept up to it and put out my hand and turned it over with a crash, and the laughter wouldn't stop.

Tommy! The goon, where'd he get to? Maybe he'd been here up until a minute or so ago. Maybe he was hiding in the cellar somewhere. I went to the door and

41

called him. No answer. I came back, ran my hand over the bulb-studded board. That sob-laughing was still sounding all around me. I wasn't doing it, was I? I shook my head to clear it and tried to think. Could that foggy fellow have forgotten to show up? *Hadn't he been here at all?*

Tuesday. Tuesday night. This was Tuesday night. Wasn't Tommy supposed to show up for the haunt tonight? That's what I thought. A vague memory flashed across my mind – Tommy telling me what night he wanted to pull his trick. He had gone, 'Wuh-Wuh-Wuh-Wuh-Wuh –' for about thirty seconds before he got it out. But a guy doesn't make that noise when he's trying to say 'Tuesday'. He does it when he's trying to say 'Wednesday'. Oh, but that was too damn silly! Whatever in the world made me think it was Tuesday? I knew he'd said something about Tue – Oh, yes! 'C-contact your snow queen on Tuesday so you'll be sure to have her at the house on Wuh-Wuh-Wuh –' That was it!

I punched myself in the mouth, I was so sore. Well, it didn't matter – some son of a gun had been monkeying with these controls for the last hour or so, and I didn't care who it was! I rushed the beam over the wiring, located the power line and tore it away from the switchboard. That would do it.

That didn't do it. First I heard that laughter, and then I heard Miriam scream. I bolted for the door – straight for the door, even though it meant ploughing through all of Tommy's electrical equipment. I hit the cellar room amid a shower of coils and broken bulbs and rheostats and headed for the stairs. As I reached them, another thought wound itself around my heart and tried to stop it. Miriam was in the first floor back room – the room into which I had carried her – the room where four people had been inexplicably but thoroughly strangled!

42

I really made time. I was running too fast to get through the door clean, and I left a piece of my shoulder on the doorpost and kept running. This was it. This was our little haunt. That house didn't need Tommy!

Miriam was lying on the divan with her head twisted crazily and blue marks on her throat.

I screamed and whirled and ran out. A doctor – a policeman – I had to get someone! Miriam – I'd done this to Miriam! If she was dead, then I killed her!

I flew down the hall, out through the foyer. The outer door stopped me for a moment because it opened inward. I wrestled it open, stood gasping at the top of the steps. This was the way it was, then. This was what had happened to Grandt, and Fortunato had found Grandt as I found Miriam. Fortunato was lucky. He broke his neck running out of the house. I wished my neck was broken, and then I wouldn't have to worry about killing Miriam. I looked hungrily down the steps. Three other men had died on them the same way – why not one more? The laughter behind me fell away and settled into a low, expectant gurgle. It wasn't going to happen again. Strangle one person, and break another's neck on the steps. That's the way it always had been. That's the –

'*No!*' I sobbed, and turned and butted my way back into the house. When I did, the laughter stopped within itself.

I went blindly back down the long corridor and into the first floor back. Miriam still lay there, and I stood, all tired inside, looking at her. I didn't want to go near, didn't want to touch, didn't want anything. I just looked at her woodenly, the way she was stretched there and twisted, the way her head hung, and the way those blue marks on her long white neck bit in and shifted and bit again. And then I saw that she hadn't been strangled at all, for – *she was being strangled!*

With a hoarse bark I leaped in, seized her, lifted her. I

43

had to pull against something. I propped her up with one arm, felt around her throat with the other hand. Nothing there! I picked her up and tried to carry her away, and I couldn't because she was being held by the neck! I clutched her to me and put everything I had into that effort to tear her away, and I couldn't! Then I felt something give, and her eyes rolled up out of sight. She looked ghastly in the crazy light from the torch that still flung its bright shaft angling upward from where I had jammed it. I knew it hurt her, and I could all but feel her pain. Then everything let go, and by a miracle I stayed on my feet, and I stumbled and bungled and carried her out of the room and out of the house and into the car.

As soon as we were well away from there I pulled over to the kerb. She couldn't have lived through that – she couldn't! But why was she moving, then, and whispering something? I pulled her to me, chafed her wrist. She was saying my name. I almost laughed. She began to swear in a deep, husky voice. I did laugh.

'Oh – boy!' she said, and licked her lips. 'Have I been through the mill!' She touched her neck weakly and grinned.

'Darling, I'm a heel to get you into that place. I don't know whatever got into me –'

'Shush,' she said, and lay back.

She was so quiet for so long that I got frightened. 'Miriam –'

'Apropos of nothing,' she said, and her voice was so strong and normal that it was a shock to me, 'there's a question you asked me that I've been dodging. I'll marry you if you like.'

I was still feeling like a heel. 'What *for*?' I asked in real amazement. She leaned over against me.

'Because,' she said softly, 'I always wanted to be married to a man who could tell me ghost stories on long winter evenings.'

There are just two more things to tell. Tommy

refused to be our best man because he was sore at me for wrecking his equipment. The other thing is that I bought the chalet on Grove Street and had it razed. We built our house there and we're very happy in it.

Slimmy Cob and his hair stood up short, tough and wiry. His eyes were slitted like his mouth, both emitting, from his dark face, thin lines of blue-white. 'Blow!' he gritted, and his finger tightened on the trigger of the snub-nosed weapon he held.

The other man in the ship raised his face by making his pillar of a neck disappear into great hunched shoulders. I was afraid of this, he thought, and his fingers froze over the control panel. 'Better put that toy away,' he said softly.

'I want a chance to unload it,' said Slimmy, and he moved the muzzle coldly across the back of Bell Bellew's hairless skull. 'And I'll sure get my chance unless you get out of that bucket seat and let me land the ship. Ain't kiddin', son.'

Bell grinned tightly, jammed his knees into the recesses provided for them under the board, and with one dazzling movement threw two switches. The gravity plates under Slimmy's feet went dead and those in the overhead whipped the little man upward. He hung there, spitting and swearing like an angry kitten. Wrenching one pinned arm away, he aimed and fired. An opaque white liquid squirted downward, lathering the big man's skull, running down over his ears and eyes, down his neck. Bell swore chokingly, clawing at his face. He felt swiftly over the panel, his practiced fingers finding the right switches as if they were tipped with eyes. Slimmy fell heavily to the deck plates, and Bell pounced on him.

Great fingers wrapped themselves around Slimmy's throat, through which gasped the words, 'Dammit! Why didn't I try to kill you outright instead of poisoning you?' His jaws champed, and his slot of a mouth closed as his slitted eyes opened wide and began to pop.

On the arid, shining planet below the silver ship, three naked, leather-skinned Martians crouched around a compact recording instrument, their implacably logical minds cubby-holing the above happenings. Their recorder, receiving by means of a tight beam vibration from the control room of the Earthlings' ship, showed in its screen every detail of the chamber, clearly-sounded every word. A slight drift of the ship above moved it away from the spy beam, and the signals faded out. One of the Martians bent swiftly to the instrument while the others spoke in their high, monotonous voices.

'They are unaccountable as ever,' said the first. His words were spoken syllable by syllable, with no emphasis on any of them, with no rise or fall of tone at the end of his sentence. The language of Mars is necessarily that way, since Martians are tone-deaf.

'It is beyond understanding,' said the other, 'that these two humans, who have come from the Solar System to this planet of Procyon, should have lived so amicably together until the day they arrived here on Artna, and then strive to kill one another.'

'At least,' said the first, 'we have discovered their purpose in coming here.'

'Yes. I trust that they will meet with no success.'

'If they fail, they will have done no more than we have. The Artnans are far from hostile, but guard their secret closely. However, it seems reasonable to me to dispatch these Earthmen. Their presence here accomplishes nothing for us.'

The third Martian turned the still-dead recording machine at this. 'I would advise against that,' he piped. 'He,' by the way, is a term of convenience. Martians are parthenogenetic, or self-germinating females. Variation of racial strains is accomplished by a periodic mutual absorption. 'Earthmen, involved and unnecessary as

47

their thought-processes are, have achieved a certain degree of development. Hampered by such inefficient and wandering mentalities, they could only have developed so far by possessing some unexplained influence over the laws of chance. Should that quality be used here, they might discover the secret we are after – how the Artnans produce U-235 so cheaply that they can undersell Martian and Terrestrial atomic fuel.'

'There is reason in that,' said the first Martian, than which there is no higher compliment to a Martian. 'If we cannot discover the secret ourselves, we may conceivably secure it from any who get it before us.' He turned back to his machine, but to no avail. The little silver ship had disappeared over the horizon, and the Martian spy ray was strictly a sight-line proposition.

When the blue began to show through Slimmy's tanned skin, Bell Bellew let go the little man's throat, took one wizened ear between each great forefinger and thumb, and began to rap on the deck plates with Slimmy's skull. A little of this, and the gun toter called it quits. Bell sat on his prostrate shipmate and grinned broadly.

'Get off,' wheezed Slimmy. 'I feel all crummy, lying under this big pile of –'

Bell put a hand under his chin and slammed the wiry head on the deck again.

'O.K. – O.K. You got me. Now what?'

'What was it you loaded that gun with?' asked Bell.

'Zinc stearate, lug, in an emulsion of carbohydrates and hydrogen oxide. I couldn't think of anything you needed more or liked less.'

'Soap and water,' nodded Bell. 'Couldn't believe it, that's all, coming from you.' He climbed off. 'Enough horseplay, little one. We got to get to work. We're over the horizon anyway. That spy ray of theirs won't see any more of this droyma.'

Slimmy got his feet under him uncertainly, and shook his spinning head. 'Now that we're here, what do we do?'

'We land as near as we can get to the Artnans' transmutation plant and see if we can get a gander at how they make U-235 out of U-238.'

'You really believe they can do that?'

'They must. I used to think they mined it, but they don't. Artna has an atmosphere much like Earth's, except that there's more xenon and neon and less nitrogen in the air. Also considerable water; and you know as well as I do that '235 can't exist where there's water.'

'I dunno,' said Slimmy. 'The fact that they produce so much, so cheaply, is a contradiction in terms. Uranium is a little more plentiful here than it is on Earth, but it has less than Mars. And the ratio of '238 to '235 is 140 to 1, same as anywhere else. Damn, boy,' he burst out suddenly, 'won't it be something if we crack this racket?'

'Sure will,' breathed Bell.

The simple words bore a weight of profound meaning, for in spite of their skylarking tendencies, Cob and Bellew never belittled the importance of their mission. Its history went back nearly five hundred years, to the ill-fated days when Earth first flung her pioneer ships out into space, to bring back their tales of other, older civilizations. They found the dead remains of the titans of Jupiter, and they brought back miles of visigraph records from the steaming swamps of Venus. But from Mars they brought undreamed-of power; a beam of broadcast energy from the old red planet that seemed inexhaustible. Earthmen were free to come and go; Earthmen saw the broadcasting towers that gave them their power, and the measureless stores of purest U-235 that fed it. The only thing they were not allowed to see was the plant which supplied the '235. Earth did not care much about that – why should they? They got power from Mars for a fraction of what it cost them to produce it themselves, so they took the Martian power and shut down their own plants.

Of course, there were one or two small rights which the Martians exacted in exchange — little matters concerning the rights to Earth's mineral resources, occasional requests to the effect that Earthmen must stop researches in certain directions, must prevent the publication of certain books, must limit their travel in certain directions — The edicts came far apart, and were applied with gentle and efficient firmness. Occasionally a group of Earthly hotheads would find reason to resent the increasing Martian influence. They were disciplined, usually by the greater mass of their own race, the hypnotized sheep who blathered of 'beneficent dictatorship'; who quoted interminably the Mars-schooled leader of men who burned his speeches into the souls of all — Hyatte Grove, who said, 'To Mars we owe our power, our transportation, our every industry. To Mars we owe our daily bread, our warless, uneventful, steadily progressive lives. The Martian power beam is the beating heart of our world!'

Earthmen outnumbered Martians ten to one. Martians outlived Earthmen eight to one. The advantage was with Mars. The Martian conquest was applied without blood, without pain. There was no war of worlds, no great fleet of ray-equipped ships. There was just the warming, friendly power beam, and the great generosity of Earth's 'Elder Sister'. Generation after generation of men lived and died, and each of them was gradually led deeper into the slow-spun web of the red planet. Earth entered into a new era, one of passive peace, submission, slavery.

Some men knew it for what it was, and did not care. Some cared, but could think of nothing to do about it. Some did something about it, and were quietly killed. Most of humanity didn't bother about what had happened. You were born and cared for. You grew up and were given a job. You were comfortable. Sometimes you were allowed to marry and have children, if it was all right with Mars. Married or single, there was room for everyone. When you were too old to be useful, you begged and were cared for by your fellows – that was easy, for everyone had so much. Then you died, and they dropped your carcass into the disintegrating furnaces. So what difference could it make whether or not man or Martian ran the show?

When man owned the Earth, you were told, he made a mess of it. No one killed now, or stole or broke any law. It was better. No one thought very deeply or clearly; no one had ambition, pride, freedom. That was better, too – for Mars. Mars grew fat on Earth's endeavour.

But some Earthmen didn't know when they were well off. They read the forbidden books, and studied the forbidden sciences, and most of them were killed off before they could add anything; but some did, and in a few centuries they had accomplished something. They knew these things:

Earth had a soul of her own, and they were determined to restore it to her.

Mars was the master – but Mars herself was a slave! And power had enslaved the red planet even as it had Earth. A thousand years and more before the first clumsy Earth ships had landed on Mars, Mars, too, had had great plants for the transmutation of '238 into '235. But one night an object was found on the Great Plain near the city of Lanamarn. It had appeared without a whisper; it was an irregular cylinder containing various simple objects – spheres, cubes, triangular and square plane surfaces of a tough alloy. Each was marked with a symbol. The Martians experimented with the things, drew some shrewd conclusions, and deposited other objects in the cylinder, replacing the cap. There was a shrill whine; on removing the cap again, the Martians found that their offerings had disappeared and were replaced by still other objects, each of which also bore a symbol.

After long and painstaking effort, a written language was established between Mars and the mystery from space which had sent the cylinder. The Martians learned that it had come from Artna, a planet of the Procyon system, and that the method of transmission was by way of the probability wave, a scientific refinement beyond the understanding of even Mars. It worked on the principle that matter cannot be destroyed; if it *is* destroyed in one portion of space, it must necessarily appear somewhere else. The transmission is instantaneous; as soon as it is negated at its source, it simply occurs at its destination.

And the Artnans had a proposition, to wit: Perhaps there was some little thing the Martians would like in return for the boron which showed up so strongly on the Artnans' teleospectographs. The Martians sent out a sample of U-238 and asked if the Artnans could transmute it, in bulk, to U-235. The Artnans could, and did. They cheerfully sent plans for the construction of a tremendous plant on the plain. U-238 was dumped into hoppers, stored by machinery in bins deep in the heart of the apparatus, and disappeared. Elsewhere in the plants, pure '235 poured out in pulverized, greenish-black abundance.

So Martian transmutation plants shut down, and Mars used Artnan atomic fuel exclusively. While boron was cheap, the arrangement was greatly to Mars' advantage. But the Artnans easily realized their advantage when they had cornered the power market, and they jumped the price. They kept it at just the level that would make it impossible for the Martians to reopen their own plants, until they had nearly exhausted the Martians' supply of both uranium and boron. They would accept no substitute for the boron; Mars faced an extreme economic reversal when the fortunate fact of communication with Earth was established. Hence Mars' economic penetration of Earth's resources; and now, Mars could afford to sit back and enjoy her position. Earthmen slaved in the boron mines; cargo after cargo of Terrestrial uranium was freighted to Mars to feed the maw of the gigantic 'transmutation' plant on the Great Plain.

All this was discovered by Earth's spies, the dozens who came back out of the hundreds of thousands that sought the information. In two centuries, nine attempts were made on Earth to design and build a ship which could travel to Procyon fast enough to spare its crew the misfortune of dying of old age before the ship reached there. Eight crews of workers were discovered and killed or dispersed, put to work in the mines by wandering, gently thorough Martian investigators. The ninth ship got away – a physical impossibility, as the Mars-hating element on Earth freely admitted. Mars gave them no permission to build and launch the little silver craft; but the Martian investigators stretched probability and did not discover the hidden factory.

Perhaps it was purposeful. Perhaps Mars was curious to know whether Earthmen could find the secret of Artnan transmutation. Mars couldn't. Even now that they had Earth's vast resources at their disposal, the Martians would be happy to free themselves from the Artnan monopoly of transmutation. They remembered with bitterness the carefully outfitted body of men who had entered the transmission chamber and had gone to Artna via the wave, in place of a scheduled cargo of boron. The Artnans, with their next shipment of '235, included the six-legged, two-foot-long body of an Artnan and a polite note thanking the Martians for the inclusion of the *corpses!* and expressing regret that no living thing could traverse space time via the wave; also

53

a reminder that the latest boron shipment was slightly overdue.

All of which flashed through Bell Bellew's mind as he stood beside Slimmy Cob and stared down at Artna. It had been a long trip – three years or so, even with the slight space warp stolen by workers in Martian shipyards. But Slimmy was good company, even if he did prefer horsing around to anything else in the world. They had both been picked for that quality, among many others. The reason was that the Martian mind is completely without humour, and the less Martians could understand the two men, the better it would be.

'Do you see what I see?' asked Slimmy after a long moment.

Bell followed the little man's pointing finger. Down in a hollow, nearly invisible from above, lay the squat shape of the Martian space cruiser.

'I do. I wouldn't worry about that, Slimmy. I expected that they'd be here.'

'Why?'

'As I told you – I don't think it was just luck that got this ship off Earth and out of our System. I think the Martians let us.'

'Yeah.' There was disbelief in Slimmy's voice. 'The Martians have always treated us that way – let us do as we pleased, when we pleased. Wipe the rest of that soap off, Bell; it's addled your brain.'

Bellew gave Slimmy a playful pat that brought him up against the opposite bulkhead, and went back to the controls. 'Let me know when you sight anything that looks like the Great Plain transmutation plant,' he said. 'We can start from there.'

The planet was but slightly larger than Earth, with an astonishingly smooth topography. There were no mountain ranges, and yet there were no true plains. The whole planet was surfaced with small rolling hillocks. Most were sandy; there was little vegetation. The

Artnans, whose metabolism was a mineral ore, had no agriculture.

After an hour or two Slimmy grunted and came away from the forward observation port, and switched on the visiplate, tuning in the buildings he had spotted. 'There she be, cap'n,' he said.

Bell studied the great pile of alloy. 'You got to give credit to those Martians,' he said. 'They certainly built theirs the spit an' image of this one.'

'Not quite,' said Slimmy, swinging the range finders. 'Look there — see that . . . that — What is it, anyway?'

'Sort of a shed,' said Bell. 'One flat building, not more than three feet high, and all of ten miles square!'

A warning signal pinged, and their eyes swivelled toward it. A yellow light blinked among the studs on the panel. 'Vibrations,' gritted Bell, and put a thousand feet of altitude under them so fast that he heard Slimmy's kneecaps crackle. They circled slowly over the shed, feeling carefully ahead of them with delicate instruments, and charted the hemisphere of tight-knit waves that roofed the flat structure.

'What is it?' asked Slimmy.

'Dunno. Let's sit down and see if we can find out.'

The ship settled down gently, her antigrav plates moaning. Bell followed the curve of the vibration field at a safe distance, and came down in a depression a hundred yards from its invisible edge.

'Air O.K.?'

'Sure,' said Slimmy. 'Just like home. Temperature's just under blood heat. Come a-walkin'!'

They strapped on side arms and went out, using the air lock for safety's sake. There didn't seem to be anything noxious in the air, but if there were, it might be smart to leave it outside the ship. Taking a bearing on a peculiar vegetation outcropping similar to scrub oak, they bore off toward the shed, both trying vainly to conceal the fact that they felt like a couple of kids let out of school. Three years is a long time to be cooped up in a small spaceship. Slimmy said in an awed voice that his legs didn't believe him, it was so long since they had walked more than twenty feet without turning a corner.

They topped a rise and stood a moment looking at the shed. It was barely visible from the ground, and there wasn't a sign of life anywhere about.

'Wonder why the sand don't drift over the thing,' said Slimmy.

'This might be why,' Bell grunted. He was staring at a line in the sand across their path. On their side of it, the sand puffed and tumbled in the light breeze. Toward the shed, however, there was apparently no moving air. 'See that line? Unless I'm 'way off my base, that's the edge of the vibration field.' He scooped up a handful of sand, stepped cautiously close to the line and tossed it. The sand fanned out, drifted over the line and – disappeared.

Slimmy tried it for himself before he commented. 'I would gather,' he said dryly, 'that the Artnans would rather not have anyone look into that shed.'

'Something like that,' said Bell. 'Look!' The crest of a nearby dune detached itself and scrabbled on six scrawny legs toward the line. It shot between the startled Earthmen, over the line, and almost to the low wall of the shed before it turned up its pointed tail and burrowed quickly under the sand.

'What was that?' asked Slimmy.

'An Artnan, from what I've heard.'

'Nasty little critter,' said Slimmy. 'Hey – the field didn't seem to bother it any, Bell.'

'So I noticed. Seems that the field has been set up for the benefit of you and me. And maybe even for our Martian friends over there.'

As they turned back toward their ship, Slimmy said pensively, 'What we just saw is justification for the Laidlaw Hypothesis, if it makes any difference to you.'

'What do you mean?'

'Speaks for itself, doesn't it? Laidlaw said that the inhabitants of any Solar System have a mutual ancestor, parallel evolutions, and similar metabolisms. You know yourself that Martians, Earthmen, Venusians and the extinct Javians are all bipeds composed mainly of hydrocarbons. That field was set up to keep such molecular structures out. The sand here is apparently something of the sort. The Artnan who ran through the field was something different. We'll catch us one sometime and find out just what makes him tick.'

'Yeah. You got something there. What interests me, though, is what's in that shed. If we guessed right about who it was put up for, then the shed must cover something they want to keep Solar noses out of. Ah — it wouldn't by any chance be what we're looking for, would it?'

Slimmy's eyes glowed. 'The transmutation plant? Could be, pal; could be. It's adjacent to the Prob.-wave transmitter. It's screened against Earth or Martian interference.'

'Huh!' Bell ran a thick forefinger up behind his ear. 'We got a problem here, little man. We toss ourselves through nine-odd light-years of space and wind up flat-footed in front of a killer-wave thrown up around a cubist's idea of a beanfield. I sort of expected a city — machinery, people, maybe.'

'It's not simple,' said Slimmy. 'Howsomever, let's see if you can make your brains go where your flat feet fear to tread. Let's go to work on the Martians. From the looks of things, they've been messing around here for quite some time.'

'Want to go right to work, don't you?' grinned Bell. 'Always wanted to get a Martian alone away from his playmates so you could tie a half hitch in his eye stalks! O.K. buddy — where do we find us one?'

'If I know Martians, there ought to be a couple sniffing around our ship by this time.'

57

There were.

They were lined up in front of the air lock, their spare bodies quivering with the palpitation peculiar to their race, and with their eye stalks pointing rigidly toward the approaching Earthmen, points together, in the well-known Martian cross-eyed stare. They had, of course, sensed the body vibrations of the men quite some time ago; the very fact that they were there meant that they were ready for a showdown.

'Hi, fellers,' said Slimmy laconically, flipping the butt of his atomic gun to make sure that it was loose in the holster.

'What are you doing here?' piped the Martian on the right.

'We're rick-bijitting for a dewjaw,' said Slimmy immediately. He had studied the masterworks of the ancients in his extreme youth, and this was a little something he remembered having seen under the heading, 'Double talk'.

'Yes,' said Bell, taking the cue. 'We willised the altibob, and no sooner did we jellik than — *boom!* here we are.'

The Martians regarded them silently. 'You do not tell the truth,' one of them said.

'It ain't a lie,' Bell dead-panned.

The evasion served its purpose, for to them, anything that was not a lie was the truth, and vice versa. Their hearing apparatus was partly sensitive to air-vibration and partly telepathic. Bell's last statement was the truth and they knew it was the truth; that convinced them. They'd die before they admitted they didn't know what the men were talking about.

'What are *you* doing here?' Slimmy countered, before their machinelike minds could work on the problem.

The Martians stiffened. 'It is not for you to ask,' said one of them.

'Aw, don't be like that, son,' drawled Bell. 'Haven't

58

Martians always told Earthmen that Mars takes only its just due, and does nothing for Earth but good?'

'Yeah,' said Slimmy. His inflection was drawn-out, lowering and meant 'That's a lot of so-and-so!'

But to the Martians 'Yeah' meant 'Yes,' and that was that. 'Why should things be different here? You don't have to hide the fact that you're looking for the same thing we are; maybe we can make a little deal.'

'Sure – come in and sit awhile!' Bell pushed past the Martians and unlatched the air lock. He knew that turning his back on the enemy was bad tactics, but it was good diplomacy. Besides, fast on their feet as Martians were, no one in the Universe could draw, aim and fire faster than Little Slimmy Cob.

Slimmy walked around the Martians, not between them, and sidled into the ship. He apparently faced the Martians merely to talk to them. 'Sure – come on in. Maybe we can give each other a hand. We can decide later what to do if we get the information we're after.'

Three sets of eye stalks intertwined briefly, and then the three spindly Martians bent and entered the silver ship.

The Martians squatted in a row against the starboard bulkhead sipping Earth's legendary cocola through glassite straws and coming as near to a feeling of well-being as was possible to these unemotional logicians. Slimmy's sharp eyes had noticed that one of them was taller than the others, the second taller than the third. Knowing that Martian names, being in the semitelepathic Martian language, were unpronounceable to humans, he had dubbed them Heaven, Its Wonders, and Hell.

'Have another coke,' said Bell heartily.

Its Wonders passed his empty flask. Bellew flashed a glance at Slimmy, and Slimmy nodded. The Martians were getting nicely mellow; a carbonated drink plasters up the Martian metabolism with amazing efficiency.

Intoxication, however, is not befuddlement to a Martian. It merely makes him move slower and think faster. If he drinks enough, he will stop altogether and turn into a genius for an hour or so. The idea of gassing the Martians up was to disarm them as to the humans' motives; for they knew that no human would dare to try to pull the wool over a drunken Martian's eyes.

The Martians accepted the drink as a gesture of good faith, for they knew that they would soon be unable to navigate. It was the pipe of peace between them, with the Earthmen paying the barkeeper, which was the way any deal with Mars seems to work out. So when the pale-blue flush began to blossom across their leathery hides, Slimmy went to work on them.

'Look fellers,' he said bluntly, 'there's no sense in our cutting each other's throats for a while yet. If you've guessed what we're here after, you've probably guessed right. We know that Martian '238 isn't transmuted into '235 on Mars. We know it's done here, in that flat building under the killer field over there. All we want to know is how it's done, and whether or not the method can be used in our System.'

'What has that to do with us?' asked Hell.

'I'll take the question as a feeler,' Bellew cut in. 'You want to find out how much else we know. All right. We know that more than half of Terrestrial and Martian industry is being diverted to the production of boron to pay for the Artnans' processing of '238. We know that Martian domina ... er ... control of the Solar System won't be complete unless and until the Artnan process of transmutation is made the property of Mars; for every indication shows that the cost of the Artnan process must be practically nothing. We know that the Martian Command did not have the process when we left the System three years ago, and we know that you don't have it yet because we wouldn't have found any Martians here if you had.'

Heaven said, 'What do you want to find the process for?'

'I might say that we on Earth would like to return to Mars some of the many kindnesses she has done us,' said Slimmy around the tongue in his cheek. 'And I might say that it's none of your damn business. I'll do neither, and simply say that I won't insult your intelligence by considering the question.'

Three sets of eye stalks fumblingly sought each other out and, intertwining, connected their owners in a swift, silent conference. Coming out of the huddle, Heaven addressed the humans. 'We have certain information bearing on the matter in hand. How can we be assured that it will be to our benefit to share it?'

Bell answered that. 'I've no idea how long you've been here, but it seems as though you haven't got on the right track yet. I don't know whether we'll be able to find the process with your information and our brains. If we can, well and good. If we can't, what have you lost?'

'We will share it,' decided Its Wonders instantly. 'All we know is this: The Artnans are a race totally unlike anything in our System. They have a mineral metabolism, feeding on ores and excreting sulphides. Their culture is beyond our understanding; they seem beyond the reach of Solar reasoning. They have made no attempt to drive us away from the planet. They have also made no attempt to communicate with us, in spite of the fact that they must know we are Martians and that it is with Martians that they trade. The vibration field around the transmutation plant cannot be penetrated by anything but light; it even excludes a spy ray. There is no way of estimating the extent of their science or their civilization. They exist mainly underground; for all we know, this may be an artificial planet. There is a possibility that their science is no more advanced than ours, but that it has simply progressed along other lines. The trade with Mars may be a major or a very minor industry with them. It is completely impossible to tell. That is all we have been able to discover.'

'That might help,' said Bellew, 'and it might not. We'll work on it. Now. There's one more little point we have to take care of. How can all concerned be sure that there is no dirty work? How do we know that we will not be killed if we get the secret; how do you know that we will not kill you for it if you beat us to the gun?'

'We can promise,' said Its Wonders in his spark-coil voice.

'Won't do, chum,' said Slimmy. 'No reflection on you, but in spite of the fact that a Martian has never been known to break his word, we don't want you establishing precedents. Bad for the racial morale. Got any other ideas?'

Bellew sometimes wished that Martians could add inflection, voice control, to their speech. You couldn't tell whether they were sore, happy, insulted – anything. He shook his head quickly at Slimmy – the little man was pushing things a little.

However, Its Wonders didn't seem annoyed by the refusal of his word. 'We could,' he said, 'destroy each other's weapons.'

'Would you agree to such a proposition?'

'Yes,' chorused the three Martians.

Bellew thought fast, then drew Slimmy aside. Not wanting to risk being overheard – no one has ever figured out just how much a Martian hears by telepathy, but it is certain that they can get nothing unless it is accompanied by the spoken word – Bellew took down a cellotab and stylus and wrote swiftly:

'Those guys are really hard up, if they'll go to those lengths. What do you think?'

'It's a good idea. Let's do it.'

'It's taking an awful chance. We can ruin their guns but no human can outrun or outwrestle a Martian.'

'We'll leave that to our brains and our ship.'

Bellew looked at Slimmy for a long moment, then turned to the Martians. 'All right, fellers. We'll do it. I think that once that's taken care of we'd do better to part company. We'll operate our way and you do anything you want to. I think the best way to handle it is to have one of you stay here with Slimmy and check over our armament. I'll go over your ship with the other two and take care of yours. We'll blast away all the artillery with side arms and then pitch the pistols into the Artnans' killer field.'

'Wait!' snapped Slimmy. 'This here-is-my-hand-my-brother stuff may be on the up-and-up, but not when it separates us.'

'Don't worry about that, chum,' said Bellew. 'While friend Hell here is wreckintg our guns, you've still got your little bean shooter. Besides, these lads need us. We'll meet you in two hours by the killer field with a bushel or two of side arms. In the meantime, take care of yourself.' Waving to the two silent Martians, he led them out.

Once they were together again in their emasculated ship, Slimmy and Bell compared notes.

'What's their ship like?' Slimmy wanted to know.

'Smooth,' said Bell. 'An Ikarion 44, with all the fixin's. Got that old-style ether-cloud steering for hyperspace travel, though — you know — the one that builds etheric resistance on one bow or the other to turn the ship when she's travelling faster than light? We can outmanoeuvre them that way if it comes to a chase.'

Slimmy grinned ruefully. 'Not so you'd notice it, chum. Hell spent a long time dismantling our bow gun and blasting the pieces one by one. Don't you fret — he had to crawl up through our steering gear to get to it, and you know Martians have photographic eyes. That bootleg ether-rudder of ours is so perfect because it's so simple, and it's the easiest thing in the world to adapt to an Ikarion. How's their spatial steering?'

63

'Same as ours,' answered Bell. 'We better find us some good luck some place. By the way – remember what Its Wonders said about the killer field's stopping a spy ray. That was a slip on his part. I got looking for one when I was busting up their big guns. They have one, sure enough – a neat little portable, sound and viviscreen; and I'll bet my back teeth it records. We got to watch our mouths.'

'Yeah.' Slimmy walked over and drew himself a flask of cocola, then came and sat on his bunk next to Bell.

Bell was surprised to find that on the way Slimmy had snatched up the cellotab and stylus. He took it, shielded it closely, and began to write as he talked about the Martian ship. In a few minutes he passed the tablet to Slimmy. It read:

'A laugh for you. Heaven and Its Wonders no sooner got out of here when they began to pump me about why you'd tried to kill me just before we landed. We were right; they saw you shooting me with the water pistol and it threw their mental reactions into six speeds at once. Couldn't understand why you didn't kill me or why I didn't kill you for trying. Suggested that if I wanted to slip you the double-x, they'd see to it that you were killed. Gave me a phial of Martian paralysis virus. Told me that if we found the Artnan secret, if I killed you with the virus I'd be protected when they brought me back to the System.'

'Yep,' said Slimmy aloud as he reached for the stylus, 'them Martians are certainly nice fellers.'

Bellew motioned to Slimmy to duck the cellotab, winked, stretched and said, 'You think we ought to grab some sleep?' in a voice dripping with exactly the opposite meaning.

Slimmy said, 'Why sure,' with admirable promptness, considering that both of them had had the sleepcentres removed from their brains by outlaw Earth surgeons in preparation for the trip.

While Slimmy pulled off his shoes, Bell went to a locker and slid two pairs of thick spectacles under his tunic, along with two discs of the same material as the lenses. He switched off the lights, pulled his own bunk out from the bulkhead over Slimmy's, dropped a pair of spectacles and a disc on the little man's chest, and rolled into bed. Both men clipped the discs to their bunklights, switched them on, and donned the glasses. Martians, possessing vision far into the ultraviolet, are blind to the reds merging into the infrared which is so prevalent on their own planet. If the spy ray was functioning — and of course it was — all the screen showed was a lot of nothing on a background of the same, and all the amplifier picked up was the tiny whisper of a busy stylus.

'Been thinking about these Artnans,' wrote Bell. 'What do you suppose is the reason for their building that transmutation shed on the surface of the planet if their civilization is underground?'

'To be near the transmitter, I'd imagine. Far as I know, a probability wave can't operate below ground.'

'Seems likely. What's your guess about the process?'

'That, bud, is our little stymie. The Martians have tested the ground right clear up to the edge of the killer field for vibrations from machinery. They heard the footsteps and the burrowing of the Artnans, and the noise from the Prob.-wave transmitter and receiver. But that's all. Artnan workers — not more than eight or ten at a time — tend whatever's in that shed. Now and then a blast of artificial wind rushes through the shed. Right afterward big suction intakes gather up a powdery material and collect it in the hoppers which feed '238 into the transmitter. Then the wind blasts back with a slightly heavier powder. There's also a little vegetative sound — spores popping and whatnot, but our Martian friends don't know whether there is some plant life in the shed or whether the vibrations come from the flora

65

outside. That's a lot of info to get from ground vibrations, but you know Martian detection instruments.'

'Wonder what the Artnans do with the boron they get from Mars?' Slimmy wrote after a silent interval.

'Eat it, I guess. For all we know, the whole set-up that has made Earth a slave and put Mars on the economic rocks may be just a sideline to the Artnans. Maybe it's candy to them, or a liquor industry. That's something we'll never know as long as the Artnans act so unsociable.'

'They don't behave like an outfit that's trying to keep a monopoly,' Slimmy scrawled. 'Seems to me their very treatment of us and the Martians is their way of telling us, "We found the process. If you want to dig it up for yourselves, go to it." They don't seem to give much of a damn whether we do or not.'

'Seems sound enough. I wish we could get some slant on their psychology. Their reasoning is so absolutely alien to anything we have in our System. Old Laidlaw was right.'

Bell handed this to Slimmy and then snatched it back excitedly. '*The Laidlaw Hypothesis!*' he underlined. 'That's the answer! Laidlaw said that each Solar System had civilizations and cultures with a common ancestor, which ancestor was peculiar to the System. For that reason there is no way of predicting in what direction a new system's fauna will evolve. The Artnans are mineral eaters, right? Then, according to Laidlaw, their plants have a corresponding metabolism, and so has every other living thing in the system! Do you see what I'm getting at?'

'No,' said Slimmy aloud, forgetting himself. Bell snatched the pad and belted the little man's mouth with it before he wrote:

'It isn't an apparatus process, dope! The Artnans don't transmute '238 into '235 by electrochemistry or radiophysics or any other process we ever heard of!

Those Artnans who work in the shed aren't scientists or even mechanics! They're *gardeners!*'

'Plants?' Slimmy's amazement dug the stylus deep into the cellotab. 'How can plants transmute one isotope into another?'

'An Artnan might like to know how an Earth plant can change light and water and minerals into cellulose,' wrote Bell. 'Now; plant or mould or fungus – what sort of a place might it come from?'

'Not here,' was Slimmy's prompt reply. 'The atmosphere is slightly humid. Water and pure '235 don't mix. Any plant that gave off atomic fuel that way would blow itself from here to Scranton. It must have been brought here from an airless planet or satellite too hot or too cold for water to exist.'

'Is there such a body in this system?'

In answer, Slimmy rolled out of his bunk and went to the chart desk, returning with a sketched astro map of the system.

'Two,' he wrote on the edge of the chart. 'This one' – an arrow indicated a large planet far away from the double sun – 'and this peanut here. A ninety-six-day year, son, and it's hot. I mean, but torrid. Don't tell me anything from there could live here, if at all.'

'Might, if it's a mould or a bacterium. Temperature wouldn't make much difference to a really simple metallic mould. It's worth a try. How do we get out there without taking our three little playmates with us?'

They thought that over for a while, and then Slimmy giggled and wrote, 'Buddy, I feel an awful attack of Martian paralysis coming on!'

Bell snapped his fingers, lay back in his bunk and roared with laughter.

Heaven, Its Wonders and Hell squatted excitedly before the portable spy-ray set in the centre of their control room, watching the scene it pictured. Slimmy's head protruded from a small iron lung built into the bulkhead, and his head was stretched back so far that the skin on his neck seemed on the breaking point. His face was bluish; there was a thin line of foam on his lips, and his breath whispered whistling through the annunciator.

'Traitorous creature,' piped Its Wonders. 'He has taken our advice and inoculated his companion with the disease.'

Heaven waved his eye stalks. 'He would not have dared to do it if he had not secured the information we seek.'

'How could he?' asked Its Wonders. 'We have taken relays on the spy ray; one of us has been watching the ship constantly. They have not left it, nor have they used any instruments.'

'Their faulty logic,' said Hell, 'has probably led them to deduce the correct answer. I have remarked before that Earthmen seem to have an astonishing ability to distort the laws of chance to their own profit.'

'It is certain that they have the secret,' said Its Wonders, 'for otherwise the large one would not have attempted to dispatch the other. Where is that Earthman, anyway?'

A loud *thuck! thuck!* answered his question, as Bell Bellew banged on the insulated gate to the Martians' air lock. Heaven reached out a long, jointless arm and pressed a panel; the door opened.

'Hey,' Bell roared before he was well into the room, 'you guys better come a-runnin'. My partner's went and got himself some Martian paralysis and he can't last much longer.' Bell permitted himself a leer.

'What has that to do with us?' Heaven wanted to know.

'Everything. He has the secret of the Artnan process. His voice is gone now; all he can do is gurgle. I ain't telepathic; you are. His gurgles ought to make some sense to you.'

'You stupid primitive,' squeaked Its Wonders. 'What do you mean by inoculating him and endangering the secret? If he dies with it, we may never discover it!'

Bell looked sheepish. 'Well, it was this way,' he said. 'Slimmy figured it all out. Said it was simple once you got the idea – one of those things that's so evident you can't see it. I asked him what it was. He wouldn't say. Said he'd tell me if his life was in danger, but not before. It was too dangerous for both of us to know. I got to thinkin'. If we go back to Earth with the secret, we'd have no chance of keeping it from Mars. Mars would take the process and kill us for our pains. Why should I get myself killed? If I tied in with you, I had your promise of protection. So I slipped him the virus, thinkin' he'd tell me the process when he knew what was the matter with him. But it hit him too fast. I can't understand a word. Come on – he may be dead before we get there!' So saying, the big Earthman turned and bolted out of the Martian ship.

The Martians held a shrill consultation and then took out after Bell, their thin claws eating up the distance. Bell was running with everything he had, but the Martians passed him before he had gone an eighth of the way. They were not even breathing hard.

Martian paralysis is sure death to the people of the red planet. When Bell got to the ship he found the three Martians pressing as close to Slimmy as they dared, which was about five feet. They were straining to hear what Slimmy was mumbling, and started annoyedly when Bell burst in.

'Get away from him,' Bell wheezed. 'Dammit, now you'll never get the information. He'd die before he'd tell it to a Martian.'

'Be quiet!' snapped Hell. 'He is too far gone for that. The paralysis strikes first at the eyes, then at the hearing. He doesn't know who is here.'

69

Slimmy's tortured voice broke from moans into words. 'Bell ... process ... electrolization of ... dying, I guess ... lousy Martian ... process ... electrolization of —' Suddenly he made a tremendous effort, lifted his head, and said in a perfectly normal, conversational tone. 'We're rick-bijitting for a dewjaw.' Then his head snapped back and he lay still.

Bell thundered over to the after bulkhead, ripped open the cold locker, and tossed three flasks of cocola to the Martians. 'Drink up,' he snapped. 'You're going to need all your brains from now on if you're going to savvy *that*.' He waved a hand toward Slimmy, who was babbling busily away about willising an altibob. The Martians sucked away eagerly at the frothy liquid, willing to do anything that would sharpen their senses.

So Slimmy muttered and the Martians guzzled, and in forty minutes Bell stopped passing out cocola and went to the iron lung and opened it, and Slimmy climbed out, rubbing his neck and cursing softly.

'That was a long haul, Bell,' he complained.

'You did fine, kid,' said Bell. 'I must remember to slip you the real thing sometime.'

'What are we going to do with these disgustingly intemperate creatures?' asked Slimmy, indicating the Martians.

They were propped up against the bulkhead, limp eye stalks registering their impotent rage. They were absolutely helpless, though their implacable brains were clicking away like high-speed calculating machines. They saw it all now.

Bell thought, and snickered. 'You stick around and watch 'em. I'm going to take a ride. I'll leave fifty gallons of coke with you. They're too plastered to keep you from opening their ugly faces and pouring more coke in. Don't let them sober up. Just keep telling them that they'll drink it or you'll drown them in it.'

Together they lifted the limp bodies and dropped

them in the sand outside the ship. 'We ought to knock them off,' said Slimmy.

'I thought of that. But if you could see farther than your excuse for your nose, you might remember that we have nothing but a shrewd guess as to the accuracy of our idea about the process. If we're wrong, these guys might come in handy again.'

'Anything you say,' said Slimmy reluctantly. 'I'll take good care of them until you get back. After that, I can't promise. Take care of yourself, incidentally.'

'Worry not, little man. Ought to be back inside of fifty hours. So long.' He slapped Slimmy's back and dived back into the ship.

The port closed with a clang, and the silver ship rose, circled twice, and dwindled to a point before it slipped under the horizon. Slimmy looked after it longingly and then turned to the helpless Martians.

'Time for your bottles, babies,' he said, and went to work pouring the cocola into their gullets.

Bell followed the planet's surface until he was sure he was out of sight of the drunken Martians, and then curved up and away into space. As soon as he was out of the planet's effective space warp, he slipped into hyperspace and travelled toward Procyon and its dark companion at many times the speed of light. Watching his chronometers closely, he spun dials and flipped switches in each phase of acceleration and deceleration, and then went spatial again not two thousand miles from the inner planet. In spite of the almost perfect physical insulation of the craft, it was already growing warmer in the control room. Bellew set up a small warp around the ship to convert the heat into light that could be sent back toward the twin suns, and then began circling the planet. Delicate instruments felt into the depths of every crater, every boiling sea of rock on the hot little world. Bell let the ship fall into an orbit, and with one eye glued to a teleospectrograph

71

and the other to his detector instruments, he searched every inch of area as it passed beneath him. The hunt didn't take long — there was uranium aplenty down there. There were great pits of U-236 and '37, something he didn't know existed in the Universe, so rare are they.

But — and his teeth flashed in a wide grin as he saw it — there were correspondingly great masses of both '238 and '235. He brought the ship close to the surface, cloaked in its light-building warp, near a fiery plain where both isotopes could be detected. Through a screened telescope he saw what he was after — a field of writhing growth, nearly hidden by a fine dust of spores. They weren't plants — they were moulds; and at enormous magnification he observed their life-cycle as they ate into the uranium, turning the rarer isotopes into their structures, throwing out all impurities, including U-235. Their rate of metabolism was astonishingly fast; and when a colony of them had exhausted all the uranium near it, the moulds cast off their spores and died. The spores, heavily encysted, drifted about in the hot gases at the surface, until the nearness of their food drew them to the planet's semi-molten surface. Then they sprouted, fed, spored and died again.

Bellew let his ship settle even more, and dropped a tube of berylusteel from the hull to a drift of spores. A few of them were drawn upward by the suction he set up; then, tube and all, he snapped the ship into space. Once out there, he experimented briefly and thoroughly with his prize. The mould certainly filled the bill. The cysts apparently could stay alive without nourishment indefinitely. They germinated readily at any temperature, as long as they were in the presence of uranium. Happily, Bellew slipped into hyperspace and drove back toward Artna.

The search of the inner planet and the capture of the

spores had taken considerably longer than Bell had expected; he was twenty hours overdue when at last he sighted the great Artnan probability wave transmitter. He cast about anxiously for the spot where he had left Slimmy and the Martians. There was nothing there but tumbled sand.

Bell flung the ship down and, through a telescope, examined the ground. There had been a scuffle, apparently, and if Bell knew Slimmy, it must have been a pip, in spite of the fact that Martians are three times as strong as any human.

'A hell of a mess,' he murmured, and swung the ship toward the hollow where lay the Martian cruiser.

Landing next to it, he hunted through Slimmy's locker until he found what he wanted, concealed in a cleverly devised secret compartment. Then he opened the air lock and strode over to the Martian ship.

The port swung open as he approached. Its Wonders stood there, apparently suffering little from what must have been quite a hangover. 'What do you want?'

'Slimmy. What have you done with him?'

'Your companion is safe. He will be returned to you alive if you give us what you went away to get.'

'You've killed him!'

Its Wonders stood aside. 'Come in and see for yourself.'

Bell pushed past him. Slimmy was there, looking very sheepish in the iron grip of the other two Martians.

'Hiya, boy,' he said.

'Slimmy! What happened?'

'What happened to you in Cincinnati that night we spent at Bert's place?'

Bellew remembered the occasion. He wasn't proud of it. He'd tried to outdrink half a dozen boron miners and had failed rather miserably. He remembered with distaste the oily feeling at the pit of his stomach, and how liquor had suddenly turned from one of the greater

73

pleasures of life into nothing more nor less than an emetic. 'What's that got to do –'

'They fooled me, that's all. After you'd been gone about eight hours or so they stopped trying not to swallow the stuff and began to get greedy. I missed the gag – I fed it to them as fast as they would take it. They all got sick. Very sick. Then they started to sober up, and I had to feed 'em more while they were still weak. Gallon for gallon, they threw off what I fed them. I don't know how they did it – they sure can take it. Anyhow, I ran plumb out of cocola. We shoulda killed 'em.'

'We will,' said Bell grimly, his jaw bunching. 'O.K., fellers – let him go now.' He reached casually into his pocket and pulled out a blued-steel automatic blaster. The Martians stiffened indignantly.

'Where did you get that?' said Heaven. 'We had your promise to allow us to destroy every weapon you had aboard. You destroyed all of ours. How is it you kept that?'

Again Bell found himself wishing that a Martian could express emotion. He'd have given anything to know just how mad the tall Martian was.

'This,' said Bellew, stepping aside to let the released Slimmy past him, 'is what we call, on Earth, an ace in the hole.'

The Martians started and stopped a concerted rush at Bell as he glanced over to see if Slimmy was safe in the silver ship, and then turned to them again.

'Nice to've known you,' he said, and backed out.

As the Earth ship rose gently away from Artna, Slimmy looked happily up from the controls. 'You know, Bell, in spite of the fact that it was a dirty trick to hold out that blaster in spite of giving our word, I'm glad you did it.'

Bellew looked at the blaster and grinned, moving toward the refuse lock. 'Swing her a little left,' he said, sighting through a port. 'You got the wrong idea, chum.'

He dropped the gun into the lock, closed the upper door, and put his hand on the dumping lever. 'We promised to let them destroy all our deadly weapons. They did. This is no blaster. It's our precious little water pistol; and am I glad to do *this!*' and he threw the lever. The gun curved down and dropped right in front of the air lock of the Martian ship. Three lanky figures pounced on it, and a jet of soapy water shot futilely up at them.

THE WORLD WELL LOST

All the world knew them as loverbirds, though they were certainly not birds, but humans. Well, say humanoids. Featherless bipeds. Their stay on earth was brief, a nine-day wonder. Any wonder that lasts nine days on an earth of orgasmic trideo shows; time-freezing pills; synapse-inverter fields which make it possible for a man to turn a sunset to perfumes, as masochist to a fur-feeler; and a thousand other euphorics — why, on such an earth, a nine-day wonder is a wonder indeed.

Like a sudden bloom across the face of the world came the peculiar magic of the loverbirds. There were loverbird songs and loverbird trinkets, loverbird hats and pins, bangles and baubles, coins and quaffs and tidbits. For there was that about the loverbirds which made a deep enchantment. No one can be told about a loverbird and feel this curious delight. Many are immune even to a solidograph. But watch loverbirds, only for a moment, and see what happens. It's the feeling you had when you were twelve, and summer-drenched, and you kissed a girl for the very first time and knew a breathlessness you were sure could never happen again. And indeed it never could — unless you watched loverbirds. Then you are spellbound for four quiet seconds, and suddenly your very heart twists, and incredulous tears sting and stay; and the very first move you make afterward, you make on tiptoe, and your first word is a whisper.

This magic came over very well on trideo, and everyone had trideo; so for a brief while the earth was enchanted.

There were only two loverbirds. They came down out of the sky in a single brassy flash, and stepped out of

76

their ship, hand in hand. Their eyes were full of wonder, each at the other, and together at the world. They seemed frozen in a full-to-bursting moment of discovery; they made way for one another gravely and with courtesy, they looked about them and in the very looking gave each other gifts — the colour of the sky, the taste of the air, the pressures of things growing and meeting and changing. They never spoke. They simply *were* together. To watch them was to know of their awestruck mounting of staircases of bird notes, of how each knew the warmth of the other as their flesh supped silently on sunlight.

They stepped from their ship, and the tall one threw a yellow powder back to it. The ship fell in upon itself and became a pile of rubble, which collapsed into a pile of gleaming sand, which slumped compactly down to dust and then to an airblown emulsion so fine that Brownian movement itself hammered it up and out and away. Anyone could see that they intended to stay. Anyone could know by simply watching them that next to their wondrous delight in each other came their delighted wonder at earth itself, everything and everybody about it.

Now, if terrestrial culture were a pyramid, at the apex (where the power is) would sit a blind man, for so constituted are we that only by blinding ourselves, bit by bit, may we rise above our fellows. The man at the apex has an immense preoccupation with the welfare of the whole, because he regards it as the source and structure of his elevation, which it is, and as an extension of himself, which it is not. It was such a man who, in the face of immeasurable evidence, chose to find a defence against loverbirds, and fed the matrices and co-ordinates of the loverbird image into the most marvellous calculator that had ever been built.

The machine sucked in symbols and raced them about, compared and waited and matched and sat still

while its bulging memory, cell by cell, was silent, was silent — and suddenly, in a far corner, resonated. It grasped this resonance in forceps made of mathematics, snatched it out (translating furiously as it snatched) and put out a fevered tongue of paper on which was typed:

DIRBANU

Now this utterly changed the complexion of things. For earth ships had ranged the cosmos far and wide, with few hindrances. Of these hindrances, all could be understood but one, and that one was Dirbanu, a transgalactic planet which shrouded itself in impenetrable fields of force whenever an earthship approached. There were other worlds which could do this, but in each case the crews knew why it was done. Dirbanu, upon discovery, had prohibited landings from the very first until an ambassador could be sent to Terra. In due time one did arrive (so reported the calculator, which was the only entity that remembered the episode) and it was obvious that Earth and Dirbanu had much in common. The ambassador, however, showed a most uncommon disdain of Earth and all its works, curled his lip and went wordlessly home, and ever since then Dirbanu had locked itself tight away from the questing Terrans.

Dirbanu thereby became of value, and fair game, but we could do nothing to ripple the bland face of her defences. As this impregnability repeatedly proved itself, Dirbanu evolved in our group mind through the usual stages of being: the Curiosity, the Mystery, the Challenge, the Enemy, the Enemy, the Enemy, the Mystery, the Curiosity, and finally That-which-is-too-far-away-to-bother-with, or the Forgotten.

And suddenly, after all this time, Earth had two genuine natives of Dirbanu aboard, entrancing the populace and giving no information. This intolerable

78

circumstance began to make itself felt throughout the world – but slowly, for this time the blind man's din was cushioned and soaked by the magic of the loverbirds. It might have taken a very long time to convince the people of the menace in their midst had there not been a truly startling development:

A direct message was received from Dirbanu.

The collective impact of loverbird material emanating from transmitters on Earth had attracted the attention of Dirbanu, which promptly informed us that the loverbirds were indeed their nationals, that in addition they were fugitives, that Dirbanu would take it ill if Earth should regard itself as a sanctuary for the criminals of Dirbanu but would, on the other hand, find it in its heart to be very pleased if Earth saw fit to return them.

So from the depths of its enchantment, Terra was able to calculate a course of action. Here at last was an opportunity to consort with Dirbanu on a friendly basis – great Dirbanu which, since it had force fields which Earth could not duplicate, must of necessity have many other things Earth could use; mighty Dirbanu before whom we could kneel in supplication (with purely-for-defence bombs hidden in our pockets) with lowered heads (making invisible the knife in our teeth) and ask for crumbs from their table (in order to extrapolate the location of their kitchens).

Thus the loverbird episode became another item in the weary procession of proofs that Terra's most reasonable intolerance can conquer practically anything, even magic.

Especially magic.

So it was that the loverbirds were arrested, that the *Starmite* 439 was fitted out as a prison ship, that a most carefully screened crew was chosen for her, and that she struck starward with the cargo that would gain us a world.

Two men were the crew — a colourful little rooster of a man and a great dun bull of a man. They were, respectively, Rootes, who was Captain and staff, and Grunty, who was midship and inboard corps. Rootes was cocky, springy, white and crisp. His hair was auburn and so were his eyes, and the eyes were hard. Grunty was a shambler with big gentle hands and heavy shoulders half as wide as Rootes was high. He should have worn a cowl and rope-belted habit. He should, perhaps, have worn a burnoose. He did neither, but the effect was there. Known only to him was the fact that words and pictures, concepts and comparisons were an endless swirling blizzard inside him. Known only to him and Rootes was the fact that he had books, and books, and books, and Rootes did not care if he had or not. Grunty he had been called since he first learned to talk, and Grunty was name enough for him. For the words in his head would not leave him except one or two at a time, with long moments between. So he had learned to condense his verbal messages to breathy grunts, and when they wouldn't condense, he said nothing.

They were primitives, both of them, which is to say that they were doers, while Modern Man is a thinker and/or a feeler. The thinkers compose new variations and permutations of euphoria, and the feelers repay the thinkers by responding to their inventions. The ships had no place for Modern Man, and Modern Man had only the most casual use for the ships.

Doers can cooperate like cam and pushrod, like ratchet and pawl, and such linkage creates a powerful bond. But Rootes and Grunty were unique among crews in that these machine parts were not interchangeable. Any good captain can command any good crew, surroundings being equivalent. But Rootes would not and could not ship out with anyone but Grunty, and Grunty was just that dependent. Grunty understood this bond, and the fact that the only way it could conceivably be

80

broken would be to explain it to Rootes. Rootes did not understand it because it never occurred to him to try, and had he tried, he would have failed, since he was inherently non-equipped for the task. Grunty knew that their unique bond was, for him, a survival matter. Rootes did not know this, and would have rejected the idea with violence.

So Rootes regarded Grunty with tolerance and a modified amusement. The modification was an inarticulate realization of Grunty's complete dependability. Grunty regarded Rootes with . . . well, with the ceaseless, silent flurry of words in his mind.

There was, beside the harmony of functions and the other link, understood only by Grunty, a third adjunct to their phenomenal efficiency as a crew. It was organic, and it had to do with the stellar drive.

Reaction engines were long forgotten. The so-called 'warp' drive was used only experimentally and on certain crash-priority war-craft where operating costs were not a factor. The *Starmite* 439 was, like most interstellar craft, powered by an RS plant. Like the transistor, the Referential Stasis generator is extremely simple to construct and very difficult indeed to explain. Its mathematics approaches mysticism and its theory contains certain impossibilities which are ignored in practice. Its effect is to shift the area of stasis of the ship and everything in it from one point of reference to another. For example, the ship at rest on the Earth's surface is in stasis in reference to the ground on which it rests. Throwing the ship into stasis in reference to the centre of the earth gives it instantly an effective speed equal to the surface velocity of the planet around its core – some one thousand miles per hour. Stasis referential to the sun moves the Earth out from under the ship at the Earth's orbital velocity. GH stasis 'moves' the ship at the angular velocity of the sun about the Galactic Hub. The galactic drift can be used, as can any simple or complex mass centre in this expanding universe. There are resultants and there are multipliers, and effective velocities can be enormous. Yet the ship is constantly in statis, so that there is never an inertia factor.

The one inconvenience of the RS drive is that shifts from one referent to another invariably black the crew out, for psychoneural reasons. The blackout period varies slightly between individuals, from one to two and a half hours. But some anomaly in Grunty's gigantic frame kept his blackout periods down to thirty or forty minutes, while Rootes was always out for two hours or more. There was that about Grunty which made moments of isolation a vital necessity, for a man must occasionally be himself, which in anyone's company Grunty was not. But after stasis shifts Grunty had an hour or so to himself while his commander lay numbly spread-eagled on the blackout couch, and he spent these in communions of his own devising. Sometimes this meant only a good book.

This, then, was the crew picked to man the prison ship. It had been together longer than any other crew in the Space Service. Its record showed a metrical efficiency and a resistance to physical and psychic debilitations previously unheard of in a trade where close confinement on long voyages had come to be regarded as a hazard. In space, shift followed shift uneventfully, and planetfall was made on schedule and without incident. In port Rootes would roar off to the fleshpots, in which he would wallow noisily until an hour before takeoff, while Grunty found, first, the business office, and next, a bookstore.

They were pleased to be chosen for the Dirbanu trip. Rootes felt no remorse at taking away Earth's new delight, since he was one of the very few who was immune to it. ('Pretty,' he said at his first encounter.) Grunty simply grunted, but then, so did everyone else.

Rootes did not notice, and Grunty did not remark upon the obvious fact that though the loverbirds' expression of awestruck wonderment in each other's presence had, if anything, intensified, their extreme pleasure in Earth and the things of Earth had vanished. They were locked, securely but comfortably, in the after cabin behind a new transparent door, so that their every move could be watched from the main cabin and control console. They sat close, with their arms about one another, and though their radiant joy in the contact never lessened, it was a shadowed pleasure, a lachrymose beauty like the wrenching music of the wailing wall.

The RS drive laid its hand on the moon and they vaulted away. Grunty came up from blackout to find it very quiet. The loverbirds lay still in each other's arms, looking very human except for the high joining of their closed eyelids, which nictated upward rather than downward like a Terran's. Rootes sprawled limply on the other couch, and Grunty nodded at the sight. He deeply appreciated the silence, since Rootes had filled the small cabin with earthy chatter about his conquests in port, detail by hairy detail, for two solid hours preceding their departure. It was a routine which Grunty found particularly wearing, partly for its content, which interested him not at all, but mostly for its inevitability. Grunty had long ago noted that these recitations, for all their detail, carried the tones of thirst rather than of satiety. He had his own conclusions about it, and, characteristically, kept them to himself. But inside, his spinning gusts of words could shape themselves well to it, and they did. 'And man, she moaned!' Rootes would chant. 'And take money? She *gave* me money. And what did I do with it? Why, I bought up some more of the same.' *And what you could buy with a shekel's worth of tenderness, my prince!* his silent words sang. '... across the floor and around the rug until, by damn, I thought we're about to climb the wall. Loaded, Grunty-boy, I tell

83

you, I was loaded!' *Poor little one* ran the hushed susurrus, *thy poverty is as great as thy joy and a tenth as great as thine empty noise.* One of Grunty's greatest pleasures was taken in the fact that this kind of huntering was limited to the first day out, with barely another word on the varied theme until the next departure, no matter how many months away that might be. *Squeak to me of love, dear mouse,* his words would chuckle. *Stand up on your cheese and nibble away at your dream.* Then, wearily, *But oh, this treasure I carry is too heavy a burden, in all its fullness, to be so tugged at by your clattering vacuum!*

Grunty left the couch and went to the controls. The preset courses checked against the indicators. He logged them and fixed the finder control to locate a certain mass-nexus in the Crab Nebula. It would chime when it was ready. He set the switch for final closing by the push-button beside his couch, and went aft to wait.

He stood watching the loverbirds because there was nothing else for him to do.

They lay quite still, but love so permeated them that their very poses expressed it. Their lax bodies yearned each to each, and the tall one's hand seemed to stream toward the fingers of his beloved, and then back again, like the riven tatters of a torn fabric straining toward oneness again. And as their mood was a sadness too, so their pose, each and both, together and singly expressed it, and singly each through the other silently spoke of the loss they had suffered, and how it ensured greater losses to come. Slowly the picture suffused Grunty's thinking, and his words picked and pierced and smoothed it down, and murmured finally, *Brush away the dusting of sadness from the future, bright ones. You've sadness enough for now. Grief should live only after it is truly born, and not before.*

His words sang,

84

Come fill the cup and in the fire of spring
Your winter garment of repentance fling.
The bird of time has but a little way
To flutter — and the bird is on the wing.

and added *Omar Khayyam, born circa 1073*, for this, too, was one of the words' functions.

And then he stiffened in horror; his great hands came up convulsively and clawed the imprisoning glass . . .

They were smiling at him.

They were smiling, and on their faces and on and about their bodies there was no sadness.

They had *heard* him!

He glanced convulsively around at the Captain's unconscious form, then back to the loverbirds.

That they should recover so swiftly from blackout was, to say the least, an intrusion; for his moments of aloneness were precious and more than precious to Grunty, and would be useless to him under the scrutiny of those jewelled eyes. But that was a minor matter compared to this other thing, this terrible fact that they *heard*.

Telepathic races were not common, but they did exist. And what he was now experiencing was what invariably happened when humans encountered one. He could only send; the loverbirds could only receive. And they *must not* receive him! No one must. No one must know what he was, what he thought. If anyone did, it would be a disaster beyond bearing. It would mean no more flights with Rootes. Which, of course, meant no flights with anyone. And how could he live — where could he go?

He turned back to the loverbirds. His lips were white and drawn back in a snarl of panic and fury. For a blood-thick moment he held their eyes. They drew closer to one another, and together sent him a radiant, anxious, friendly look that made him grind his teeth.

Then, at the console, the finder chimed.

Grunty turned slowly from the transparent door and went to his couch. He lay down and poised his thumb over the push-button.

He *hated* the loverbirds, and there was no joy in him. He pressed the button, the ship slid into a new stasis, and he blacked out.

The time passed.

'Grunty!'

'?'

'You feed them this shift?'

'Nuh.'

'Last shift?'

'Nuh.'

'What the hell's the matter with you, y'big dumb bastich? What you expect them to live on?'

Grunty sent a look of roiling hatred aft. 'Love,' he said.

'Feed 'em,' snapped Rootes.

Wordlessly Grunty went about preparing a meal for the prisoners. Rootes stood in the middle of the cabin, his hard small fists on his hips, his gleaming auburn head tilted to one side, and watched every move. 'I didn't used to have to tell you anything,' he growled, half pugnaciously, half worriedly. 'You sick?'

Grunty shook his head. He twisted the tops of two cans and set them aside to heat themselves, and took down the water suckers.

'You got it in for these honeymooners or something?'

Grunty averted his face.

'We get them to Dirbanu alive and healthy, hear me? They get sick, you get sick, by God. I'll see to that. Don't give me trouble, Grunty. I'll take it out on you. I never whipped you yet, but I will.'

Grunty carried the tray aft. 'You hear me?' Rootes yelled.

Grunty nodded without looking at him. He touched the control and a small communication window slid open in the glass wall. He slid the tray through. The taller loverbird stepped forward and took it eagerly, gracefully, and gave him a dazzling smile of thanks. Grunty growled low in his throat like a carnivore. The loverbird carried the food back to the couch and they began to eat, feeding each other little morsels.

A new stasis, and Grunty came fighting up out of blackness. He sat up abruptly, glanced around the ship. The Captain was sprawled out across the cushions, his compact body and outflung arm forming the poured-out, spring-steel laxness usually seen only in sleeping cats. The loverbirds, even in deep unconsciousness, lay like hardly separate parts of something whole, the small one on the couch, the tall one on the deck, prone, reaching, supplicating.

Grunty snorted and hove to his feet. He crossed the cabin and stood looking down on Rootes.

The hummingbird is a yellow-jacket, said his words. *Buzz and dart, hiss and flash away. Swift and hurtful, hurtful . . .*

He stood for a long moment, his great shoulder muscles working one against the other, and his mouth trembled.

He looked at the loverbirds, who were still motionless. His eyes slowly narrowed.

His words tumbled and climbed, and ordered themselves:

> *I through love have learned three things,*
> *Sorrow, sin and death it brings.*
> *Yet day by day my heart within*
> *Dares shame and sorrow, death and sin. . . .*

And dutifully he added *Samuel Ferguson, born 1810.* He glared at the loverbirds, and brought his fist into his

87

palm with a sound like a club on an anthill. They had heard him again, and this time they did not smile, but looked into each other's eyes and then turned together to regard him, nodding gravely.

Rootes went through Grunty's books, leafing and casting aside. He had never touched them before. 'Buncha crap,' he jeered. 'Garden of the Plynck. Wind in the Willows. Worm Ouroborous. Kid stuff.'

Grunty lumbered across and patiently gathered up the books the Captain had flung aside, putting them one by one back into their places, stroking them as if they had been bruised.

'Isn't there nothing in here with pictures?'

Grunty regarded him silently for a moment and then took down a tall volume. The Captain snatched it, leafed through it. 'Mountains,' he growled. 'Old houses.' He leafed. 'Damn boats.' He smashed the book to the deck. 'Haven't you got *any* of what I want?'

Grunty waited attentively.

'Do I have to draw a diagram?' the Captain roared. 'Got that ol' itch, Grunty. You wouldn't know. I feel like looking at pictures, get what I mean?'

Grunty stared at him, utterly without expression, but deep within him a panic squirmed. The Captain never, *never* behaved like this in mid-voyage. It was going to get worse, he realized. Much worse. And quickly.

He shot the loverbirds a vicious, hate-filled glance. If they weren't aboard . . .

There could be no waiting. Not now. Something had to be done. Something . . .

'Come on, come on,' said Rootes. 'Goddlemighty Godfrey, even a deadbutt like you must have *something* for kicks.'

Grunty turned away from him, squeezed his eyes closed for a tortured second, then pulled himself together. He ran his hand over the books, hesitated, and finally brought out a large, heavy one. He handed it to the Captain and went forward to the console. He slumped down there over the file of computer tapes, pretending to be busy.

The Captain sprawled on to Grunty's couch and opened the book. 'Michelangelo, what the hell,' he growled. He grunted, almost like his shipmate. 'Statues,' he half-whispered, in withering scorn. But he ogled and leafed at last, and was quiet.

The loverbirds looked at him with a sad tenderness, and then together sent beseeching glances at Grunty's angry back.

The matrix-pattern for Terra slipped through Grunty's fingers, and he suddenly tore the tape across, and across again. A filthy place, Terra. *There is nothing*, he thought, *like the conservatism of license*. Given a culture of sybaritics, with an endless choice of mechanical titillations, and you have a people of unbreakable and hidebound formality, a people with few but massive taboos, a shockable, narrow, prissy people obeying the rules – even the rules of their calculated depravities – and protecting their treasured, specialized pruderies. In such a group there are words one may not use for fear of their fanged laughter, colours one may not wear, gestures and intonations one must forego, on pain of being torn to pieces. The rules are complex and absolute, and in such a place one's heart may not sing lest, through its warm free joyousness, it betrays one.

And if you must have joy of such a nature, if you must be free to be your pressured self, then off to space ... off to the glittering black lonelinesses. And let the days go by, and let the time pass, and huddle beneath your impenetrable integument, and wait, and wait, and every once in a long while you will have that moment of lonely consciousness when there is no one around to see; and then it may burst from you and you may dance, or cry, or twist the hair on your head till your eyeballs blaze, or do any of the other things your so unfashionable nature thirstily demands.

It took Grunty half a lifetime to find this freedom. No price would be too great to keep it. Not lives, nor interplanetary diplomacy, nor Earth itself were worth such a frightful loss.

He would lose it if anyone knew, and the loverbirds knew.

He pressed his heavy hands together until the knuckles crackled. Dirbanu, reading it all from the ardent minds of the loverbirds; Dirbanu flashing the news across the stars; the roar of reaction, and then Rootes, Rootes, when the huge and ugly impact washed over him . . .

So let Dirbanu be offended. Let Terra accuse this ship of fumbling, even of treachery — anything but the withering news the loverbirds had stolen.

Another new stasis, and Grunty's first thought as he came alive in the silent ship was *It has to be soon.*

He rolled off the couch and glared at the unconscious loverbirds. The helpless loverbirds.

Smash their heads in.

Then Rootes . . . what to tell Rootes?

The loverbirds attacked him, tried to seize the ship?

He shook his head like a bear in a beehive. Rootes would never believe that. Even if the loverbirds could open the door, which they could not, it was more than ridiculous to imagine those two bright and slender things attacking anyone — especially not so rugged and massive an opponent.

Poison? No — there was nothing in the efficient, unfailingly beneficial food stores that might help.

His glance strayed to the Captain, and he stopped breathing.

Of course!

90

He ran to the Captain's personal lockers. He should have known that such a cocky little hound as Rootes could not live, could not strut and prance as he did unless he had a weapon. And if it was the kind of weapon that such a man would characteristically choose –

A movement caught his eye as he searched.

The loverbirds were awake.

That wouldn't matter.

He laughed at them, a flashing, ugly laugh. They cowered close together and their eyes grew very bright.

They knew.

He was aware that they were suddenly very busy, as busy as he. And then he found the gun.

It was a snug little thing, smooth and intimate in his hand. It was exactly what he had guessed, what he had hoped for – just what he needed. It was silent. It would leave no mark. It need not even be aimed carefully. Just a touch of its feral radiation and throughout the body, the axones suddenly refuse to propagate nerve impulses. No thought leaves the brain, no slightest contraction of heart or lung occurs again, ever. And afterward, no sign remains that a weapon has been used.

He went to the serving window with the gun in his hand. *When he wakes, you will be dead,* he thought. *Couldn't recover from stasis blackout. Too bad. But no one's to blame, hm? We never had Dirbanu passengers before. So how could we know?*

The loverbirds, instead of flinching, were crowding close to the window, their faces beseeching, their delicate hands signing and signalling, frantically trying to convey something.

He touched the control, and the panel slid back.

The taller loverbird held up something as if it would shield him. The other pointed at it, nodded urgently, and gave him one of those accursed, hauntingly sweet smiles.

Grunty put up his hand to sweep the thing aside, and then checked himself.

It was only a piece of paper.

All the cruelty of humanity rose up in Grunty. *A species that can't protect itself doesn't deserve to live.* He raised the gun.

And then he saw the pictures.

Economical and accurate, and, for all their subject, done with the ineffable grace of the loverbirds themselves, the pictures showed three figures:

Grunty himself, hulking, impassive, the eyes glowing, the tree-trunk legs and hunched shoulders.

Rootes, in a pose so characteristic and so cleverly done that Grunty gasped. Crisp and clean, Rootes' image had one foot up on a chair, both elbows on the high knee, the head half turned. The eyes fairly sparkled from the paper.

And a girl.

She was beautiful. She stood with her arms behind her, her feet slightly apart, her face down a little. She was deep-eyed, pensive, and to see her was to be silent, to wait for those downcast lids to lift and break the spell.

Grunty frowned and faltered. He lifted a puzzled gaze from these exquisite renderings to the loverbirds, and met the appeal, the earnest, eager, hopeful faces.

The lovebird put a second paper against the glass.

There were the same three figures, identical in every respect to the previous ones, except for one detail; they were all naked.

He wondered how they knew human anatomy so meticulously.

Before he could react, still another sheet went up.

The loverbirds, this time — the tall one, the shorter one, hand in hand. And next to them a third figure, somewhat similar, but tiny, very round, and with grotesquely short arms.

92

Grunty stared at the three sheets, one after the other. There was something ... something ...

And then the loverbird put up the fourth sketch, and slowly, slowly, Grunty began to understand. In the last picture, the loverbirds were shown exactly as before, except that they were naked, and so was the small creature beside them. He had never seen loverbirds naked before. Possibly no one had.

Slowly he lowered the gun. He began to laugh. He reached through the window and took both the loverbirds' hands in one of his, and they laughed with him.

Rootes stretched easily with his eyes closed, pressed his face down into the couch, and rolled over. He dropped his feet to the deck, held his head in his hands and yawned. Only then did he realize that Grunty was standing just before him.

'What's the matter with you?'

He followed Grunty's grim gaze.

The glass door stood open.

Rootes bounced to his feet as if the couch had turned white-hot. 'Where — what —'

Grunty's crag of a face was turned to the starboard bulkhead. Rootes spun to it, balanced on the balls of his feet as if he were boxing. His smooth face gleamed in the red glow of the light over the airlock.

'The lifeboat ... you mean they took the lifeboat? They got away?'

Grunty nodded.

Rootes held his head. 'Oh, fine,' he moaned. He whipped around to Grunty. 'And where the hell were you when this happened?'

'Here.'

'Well, what in God's name happened?' Rootes was on the trembling edge of foaming hysteria.

Grunty thumped his chest.

'You're not trying to tell me you let them go?'

93

Grunty nodded, and waited — not for very long.

'I'm going to burn you down,' Rootes raged. 'I'm going to break you so low you'll have to climb for twelve years before you get a barracks to sweep. And after I get done with you I'll turn you over to the Service. What do you think they'll do to you? What do you think they're going to do to *me*?'

He leapt at Grunty and struck him a hard, cutting blow to the cheek. Grunty kept his hands down and made no attempt to avoid the fist. He stood immovable, and waited.

'Maybe those were criminals, but they were Dirbanu nationals,' Rootes roared when he could get his breath. 'How are we going to explain this to Dirbanu? Do you realize this could mean war?'

Grunty shook his head.

'What do you mean? You know something. You better talk while you can. Come on, bright boy — what are we going to tell Dirbanu?'

Grunty pointed at the empty cell. 'Dead,' he said.

'What good will it do us to say they're dead? They're not. They'll show up again some day, and —'

Grunty shook his head. He pointed to the star chart. Dirbanu showed as the nearest body. There was no livable planet within thousands of parsecs.

'They didn't go to Dirbanu!'

'Nuh.'

'Damn it, it's like pulling rivets to get anything out of you. In that lifeboat they go to Dirbanu — which they won't — or they head out, maybe for years, to the Rim stars. That's all they can do!'

Grunty nodded.

'And you think Dirbanu won't track them, won't bring 'em down?'

'No ships.'

'They have ships!'

'Nuh.'

94

'The loverbirds told you?'

Grunty agreed.

'You mean their own ship that they destroyed, and the one the ambassador used were all they had?'

'Yuh.'

Rootes strode up and back. 'I don't get it. I don't begin to get it. What did you do it for, Grunty?'

Grunty stood for a moment, watching Rootes' face. Then he went to the computing desk. Rootes had no choice but to follow. Grunty spread out the four drawings.'

'What this? Who drew these? *Them?* What do you know. *Damn!* Who is the chick?'

Grunty patiently indicated all of the pictures in one sweep. Rootes looked at him, puzzled, looked at one of Grunty's eyes, then the other, shook his head, and applied himself to the pictures again. 'This is more like it,' he murmured. 'Wish I'd a' known they could draw like this.' Again Grunty drew his attention to all the pictures and away from the single drawing that fascinated him.

'There's you, there's me. Right? Then this chick. Now, here we are again, all buff naked. Damn, what a carcass. All right, all right, I'm going on. Now, this is the prisoners, right? And who's the little fat one?'

Grunty pushed the fourth sheet over. 'Oh,' said Rootes. 'Here everybody's naked too. Hm.'

He yelped suddenly and bent close. Then he rapidly eyed all four sheets in sequence. His face began to get red. He gave the fourth picture a long, close scrutiny. Finally he put his finger on the sketch of the round little alien. 'This is . . . a . . . a Dirbanu —'

Grunty nodded. 'Female.'

'Then those two — they were —'

Grunty nodded.

'So that's it!' Rootes fairly shrieked in fury. 'You mean we been shipped out all this time with a coupla

95

God damned *fairies*? Why, if I'd a' known that I'd a' killed 'em!'

'Yuh.'

Rootes looked up at him with a growing respect and considerable amusement. 'So you got rid of 'em so's I wouldn't kill 'em and mess everything up?' He scratched his head. 'Well, I'll be billy-be-damned. You got a think-tank on you after all. Anything I can't stand, it's a fruit.'

Grunty nodded.

'God,' said Rootes. 'It figures. It really figures. Their females don't look anything like the males. Compared with them, our females are practically identical to us. So the ambassador comes, and sees what looks like a planet full of queers. He knows better but he can't stand the sight. So back he goes to Dirbanu, and Earth gets brushed off.'

Grunty nodded.

'Then these pansies here run off to Earth, figuring they'll be at home. They damn near made it, too. But Dirbanu calls 'em back, not wanting the likes of them representing their planet. I don't blame 'em a bit. How would you feel if the only Terran on Dirbanu was a fluff? Wouldn't you want him out of there, but quick?'

Grunty said nothing.

'And now,' said Rootes, 'we better give Dirbanu the good news.'

He went forward to the communicator.

It took a surprisingly short time to contact the shrouded planet. Dirbanu acknowledged and coded out a greeting. The decoder over the console printed the message for them:

GREETINGS STARMITE 439. ESTABLISH ORBIT. CAN YOU DROP PRISONERS TO DIRBANU? NEVER MIND PARACHUTE.

'Whew,' said Rootes. 'Nice people. Hey, you notice they don't say come on in. They never expected to let us land. Well, what'll we tell 'em about their lavender lads?'

'Dead,' said Grunty.

'Yeah,' said Rootes. 'That's what they want anyway.' He sent rapidly.

In a few minutes the response clattered out of the decoder.

STAND BY FOR TELEPATH SWEEP. WE MUST CHECK. PRISONERS MAY BE PRETENDING DEATH.

'Oh-oh,' said the Captain. 'This is where the bottom drops out.'

'Nuh,' said Grunty, calmly.

'But their detector will locate – oh – I see what you're driving at. No life, no signal. Same as if they weren't here at all.'

'Yuh.'

The coder clattered.

DIRBANU GRATEFUL. CONSIDER MISSION COMPLETE. DO NOT WANT BODIES. YOU MAY EAT THEM.

Rootes retched. Grunty said, 'Custom.'

The decoder kept clattering.

NOW READY FOR RECIPROCAL AGREEMENT WITH TERRA.

'We go home in a blaze of glory,' Rootes exulted. He sent,

TERRA ALSO READY. WHAT DO YOU SUGGEST?

The decoder paused, then:

TERRA STAY AWAY FROM DIRBANU AND DIRBANU WILL STAY AWAY FROM TERRA. THIS IS NOT A SUGGESTION. TAKES EFFECT IMMEDIATELY.

'Why that bunch of bastards!'

Rootes pounded his codewriter, and although they circled the planet at a respectful distance for nearly four days, they received no further response.

The last thing Rootes had said before they established the first stasis on the way home was: 'Well, anyway – it does me good to think of those two queens

97

crawling away in that lifeboat. Why, they can't even starve to death. They'll be cooped up there for *years* before they get anywhere they can sit down.'

It still rang in Grunty's mind as he shook off the blackout. He glanced aft to the glass partition and smiled reminiscently. 'For years,' he murmured. His words curled up and spun, and said,

> *... Yes; love requires the focal space*
> *Of recollection or of hope,*
> *Ere it can measure its own scope.*
> *Too soon, too soon comes death to show*
> *We love more deeply than we know!*

Dutifully, then, came the words: *Coventry Patmore, born 1823.*

He rose slowly and stretched, revelling in his precious privacy. He crossed to the other couch and sat down on the edge of it.

For a time he watched the Captain's unconscious face, reading it with great tenderness and utmost attention, like a mother with an infant.

His words said, *Why must we love where the lightning strikes, and not where we choose?*

And they said, *But I'm glad it's you, little prince. I'm glad it's you.*

He put out his huge hand and, with a feather touch, stroked the sleeping lips.

THE POD AND THE BARRIER

A lousy mission.

Of course, it was a volunteer (i.e., suicide) mission, and for that you take what comes. They may wine you and dine you and honour you and your tribe for three generations coming and going, in the days before you start. But once you're on your way, you can't expect it to be a pleasure. Everything about suicide is death, not just the final part.

Potter picked his nose and didn't know he was doing it, even while he was looking you straight in the eye, talking to you at the time. Try shipping out with that. That's what bothered me the most, anyway. Most of the others seemed to be bugged by Donato. He had a psychosomatic cough that passed all the preflight medics for the simple reason that he had never had such a thing before, probably because he had never gone out to die before. Me, I guess I have soaked up enough of that 'profound compassion' of the Luanae to defend me against that kind of annoyance. But Potter the Picker, now – that got to me, I admit it.

Then there was little Donato, always trying to please. Some people are annoying because once in a while they just don't go out of their way to make things a little happier for anyone else. Donato hit the other extreme, always making way, never disagreeing, forever finding some way to help or get a cushion to move back or bring or say or not say whatever anyone else might want, until you wanted to scuttle the ship just so it would take him with the lot of you. The main trouble was, he was so helpful he never gave you anything to complain about. Time after time I would see one or the other of the crew suddenly wheel on him out of a dead silence and roar at him to get the hell out. 'Why sure, friend,' he'd always say, and smile, and get the hell out, leaving whoever it was beating himself on the temples.

Potter was a specialist in field mechanics and Donato was a top ballistics man. England was an ugly man with big ears and wet eyes who kept to himself pretty much only he ate loud. He was an expert in missile control. And I'm Palmer; I heard there was a man in Alpha Sigma IV once who knew more about transspatial stress than I do, but I don't believe it. The four of us had four different ideas for breaking the Luanae Barrier, and that's what we were on our way to do. All four ideas were pretty farfetched, and the odds were much in favour of the Barrier's getting us, but it had to be done. After everything reasonable has been tried on something that must be done but can't be done, you have to start calling in the crackpots. I had to bring along my perfectly valid theories with the three crackpots because it was the only way they would ever get tried.

And that was the expedition personnel. The others were just operations. A skipper, Captain Steev, strictly ferryboat, who knew everything he had to know about running the ship and getting her there, and didn't know, didn't care, wouldn't talk about anything else. Some of the others griped about the kind of skipper we had, but not me. He had to be expendable and he was. He had to know his job and he did. So?

The utility monkey was funny for about half an hour of anybody's time, and forever after that just unpleasant to have around. He was sort of misshapen, with a head much too big for his body and a left leg with too much bounce in it. It's been so many hundreds of years, I guess, since anyone had anything drastic wrong with him physically, that nobody can get used to it any more. You know how to be polite about it when you do encounter it, and back home you know how to forget you saw it pretty thoroughly, but on a space you can

100

never get the chance. Personally, I think we should have shipped without a utility man. I don't know if I feel so strongly about it that I'd have done the dirty work on the ship myself, but maybe one of the others would. I don't care how much humanity progresses, there is always a little room somewhere for the unskilled hand, lifting and mopping and cleaning out the sewer lines when something gets stuck. This monkey we had went by the name of Nils Blum, and nobody paid much attention to him.

And then we had the unemployed CG. Did you ever hear of an unemployed Crew's Girl – on a ship? I don't mean kicking around the spaceports waiting to ship out, unemployed that way. I mean right there aboard, she had nothing to do. CG's as a whole are a dowdy bunch. There's no point in putting cute clothes, cute tricks, and heady perfume aboard a space can. You don't need to stimulate anything; that takes care of itself as time goes by. They keep themselves clean and wait around till they're needed. They're a thick-skinned, slow-witted lot because there's no sense in sensitivity in their line; it just makes trouble. This Virginia we shipped, she came from the bottom of the underside of the sump. She was everything that distinguishes a CG from a real earthside female woman. She had a wide face that was closed and bland as a bank-vault door on the Sabbath, and a build that was neither this nor that but sort of statistically there. With a normal personality, or none at all, she might have had a job to do, and would have done it. But with the personality she had ... well, at first you just didn't like her and after a while you couldn't stand her, and finally you got the feeling about her that she was a lower animal, that you couldn't stand what the others might think of you if you went near her. There was a lot of difference of opinion aboard on a lot of subjects, but not on that one. So that's what we had, believe it or not, an unemployed CG. I read someplace about an Arctic explorer back in the days where the poles of Old Earth were covered with ice. He used to bring along the ugliest woman he could find to cook. Her other function was to inform him when he'd been away from civilization too long, which she did by beginning to look good to him. Well, maybe given time enough, we'd have found something for this Virginia to do. But given that much time, we'd all be dead. Oh, she was a great help aboard, Virginia was.

That personality. I thought a lot about that personality of hers, just because on a long haul you have time to think a lot about everything. I knew a kid in school who had a face so insulting, so all-fired arrogant when it was relaxed that the teachers used to throw him out of the class just for sitting there, at least until they learned what the trouble was and had him remodelled. Well, maybe Virginia's personality was something like that. Maybe she couldn't help it. She had a way of carrying a cloud of what Potter once called 'retroactive doubt'. When she was anywhere near you, you breathed it. You'd say something and she would repeat it, and by the way she did it — I can't describe it at all, but I'm telling you the truth — by the way she did it, she made whatever you'd said into a falsehood. Sometimes it suddenly sounded like a lie and sometimes like a mistake and sometimes like something you could be expected to believe because you were ignorant. I mean, just by repeating your very own words she would do this. You'd say, 'Back home I've got a silver-headed walking stick,' and she'd say, 'Yeah, you've got a silver-headed walking stick,' in that dull flat drone of hers, and by damn you'd find yourself arguing with her that you *did* have one; I mean fighting, defending yourself, the way you only can when you doubt something yourself. Then she'd go away and you'd sit and stew about the walking stick, wondering where it was you last saw it, wondering if you really did have it any more, if the head of it was real silver. It didn't have to be something that was important at all; she could make you feel that way. When it *was* important . . . shipmate, better not mention it around her. I think you could tell her your name and she'd make you doubt it. As a matter of fact, now I think of it, she did just that to me, the day I first saw her (which is traditionally the day after upship). I walked up to her in the messhall and said, 'My name's Palmer,' and she looked at me without blinking and said flatly, 'Your name's Palmer,' and made me say, before I could stop myself, 'No – really it is,' and then skulk off feeling damn strange.

We'd taken off with a null-grav tug and slipped into second-order matrix within six hours – all very fast and painless, thanks to the Luanae. Both devices were theirs, and so was the ship's power plant, and so was the subetheric communication we could get loud and clear for almost four full days after upship. Do you know how far that would be in miles? Frankly, I don't, but four days is enough to take you halfway to Sirius, and that's a powerful long reach for a communicator phasing out of normal space and finding your receiver. I recall especially that fourth day's bulletins, because we all gathered around to soak them up and chew them thoroughly; we knew that we'd hear nothing else from the Earth Worlds from there on for the six ship-weeks it took us to get out to the Luanae Barrier, 'way out on the other side of the Coalsack. We cheered the whiffleball scores and the chess results and laughed too loud at the human-interest bit about the kid who brought the Nova Mars stink-dog into school; and then there was the last real news we heard, that Chicago had been frozen from the Northern Ontario Parish clear south to the Joplin city limits, back on Old Earth.

Everybody tsk-tsked.

'Well,' said Potter, looking at his finger, 'I guess there's no other way.'

'But people always get killed in a freeze,' said big-eared England.

'More people get killed in a riot,' I remember saying.

About then the signal faded, very abruptly as it does when you get out of range in subspace, and we all sat around worrying a bit. It was funny, that news of all news being the last we heard. It was like a nudge, a sendoff. A reminder. Old Earth wasn't the only place where there were riots, not by a sight. Of eighteen planets in the two so-called Earth Galaxies, only Ragnarok and Luna-Luna were not bulging at the seams, and they'd be as bad as the others in a generation. By and large people behaved themselves ... but there were so *many* of them! The law of averages dictated that in that number there had to be so many trouble-makers, there were bound to be so many riots — and there had to be more all the time.

Unless we broke the Luanae Barrier.

We owed the Luanae a lot. As I said before, a good deal of our most advanced technology is built on transmissions from the Luanae. A very old people, ancient before old Sol the First was a sun. Wise and compassionate. That was the real cliché, the compassionate Luanae. True enough, though. No one had ever seen them, of course — the Barrier took care of that. No one understood the exact method of their transmissions, though they tried their best to explain. You'd get in range and then there it was, they were talking to you, inside your head. What they said was true — that you could bank on, swear by, hang your hat or your life on. Some things have to be proved. Not anything the Luanae said, though. You might not believe it if you heard about something they said, from me, say. But go hear it from them — you'll *know* it's so. Never in the three hundred years of contact had anything they said turned out to be anything but exactly so. They say that at first humanity took it with a dose of salts — we are a suspicious species. But although the Luanae couldn't give us the specs of a machine like theirs – they insisted that their transmitter was only a machine – they were able to describe an odd little recorder that would play back and 'sound' like the original. When a few million of those had been made and distributed, there wasn't any suspicion any more. It just blew away.

But population-pressure rioting isn't as easy to dispose of as inbred suspicion. Put enough people in a limited ground, and you'll have trouble. Put too much in the same ground, and – look out. Now we had sixteen worlds with too much humanity, and two more with almost enough to start trouble. And all we could do was watch and feel, and freeze whole areas when the thing boiled over. After the freeze, the United Planet men would spread through the countryside, picking up the mangled corpses from ground-cars and aircraft which had smashed up when everyone blacked out, and making the millions of others comfortable where they lay. They'd wake up in due course, with no sense of time passed, but the dead would have been long buried and the trouble-makers located and treated, and the immediate causes of the riot, whatever they might be (it didn't take much) adjudicated and put right. It was generally suspected that the UP boys declared riot and froze areas on somewhat less excuse than they really needed, but most people didn't object. At least it kept a few million people, each time, from breeding any more for six to eight months. But nobody denied that this was pure stopgap. As to halting reproduction altogether for a while, the suggestion came up monotonously in the Council sessions, and was as monotonously knocked down. Enforced sterility is counter to the most basic of civil rights, and the Earth Worlds would die before they would relinquish any basic right.

They were dying, too.

And there, hanging just out of reach, were the

Luanae Earths — eight fine Earth-type planets circling three suns in Galaxy Three. Eight beautiful worlds, ready and waiting; we wanted them and the Luanae wanted us to have them. And all we could do was watch them swing by and feel wistful, because of the Barrier.

The Luanae are not terrestrial. As far as can be understood, they have a boron metabolism, and compete in no way with us hydrocarbon types. They need nothing from us, and wouldn't take it if they did need it. When they say they have those worlds to give us, when they say they're suitable, when they say for sure that they are the only planets left in this entire quadrant of the universe — why, you can bet on it. (They're the ones who found Luna-Luna and Ragnarok for us, when the Earth Worlds had despaired of ever finding another terrestrial planet.) We also have their assurance that in the other quadrants are literally thousands of terrestrial planets; but we will need a totally new technology to reach them, and that will take us maybe four centuries to acquire, even with their help. Well, the Earth Worlds wouldn't last four centuries without the Luanae planets. With them, though — with them, it might be done. All we had to do was reach them. All we had to do was penetrate the Barrier.

The Barrier was a sphere in space — not a thing, exactly; just a place which could be represented on a cosmimap as a sphere. It was a fair-sized sphere; it englobed a third of the Luanae galaxy, including of course the three little Luanae home-planets, and the eight lovely unreachable Luanae Terrestrials. All it did, that Barrier, was to draw a line. Anything outside of it was left strictly alone. Anything penetrating it was instantly tracked, hunted and smashed by Luanae missiles. And anything that got cute enough to duck inside and out again was destroyed by the Barrier itself, which had the simple ability of reversing the terrene-sign of a random third of the atoms in any matter it touched. You can imagine what happened to anything from a micrometeorite to a sun that got exposed to it. Shot through and through with contraterrene matter. Disappeared in a single ferocious flash.

The Luanae galaxy was discovered three hundred years ago by a creaky old Earth survey ship powered by Teller-formula atomics and a primitive subspace drive which barely quadrupled effective light-velocity. The first thing the ship – it was called the *Luanae*, after its skipper's wife and daughter, both of whom were named Luana – the first thing they saw was the Luanae galaxy, a long narrow elliptical one with a dark band, the perfect arc of a circle, a third of the way down the long axis. It looked artificial, so they hobbled over there to investigate. It was artificial all right. It was the Barrier, or rather, the segment of space through which the Barrier had removed all impinging matter. And when they got within a dozen light-years of it, they were in range of the beings who came to be known by the same name as the ship and the galaxy – the Luanae.

They said *Stop*.

They said it simultaneously inside the heads of everyone aboard. They said it with that encasement of utter truth and total believability. They said it (they told us later) with an automatic machine set up aeons ago, to warn away any intelligent life from their Barrier. But when the ship *Luanae* responded (by stopping) it wasn't any machine that spoke next. The strange creatures set up such a welcome, such a warm, admiring, congratulatory flood of thought that they say all hands looked at each other in amazement and started to weep. And along with the welcome – a warning. *Don't come any closer*. They threw a few million cubic metres of rubble up from the inside of the Barrier and let the astonished crew watch the near margins of the invisible Barrier light up with a hellish three-hour show of destruction. They urged experiment, suggesting that the survey ship throw something at the Barrier. The ship did. Whatever matter penetrated was overtaken and destroyed by what appeared to be tiny hunting missiles. Whatever matter was angled through the Barrier's skin so that it would cut a chord and emerge again, flowered into flame as it left. The men on the ship knew, down to the marrow, that they were welcome — thirstily, ardently welcome. And they knew they were warned.

The ship hung outside the Barrier for more than a year, setting down what turned out to be the greatest treasure ever brought home by a vessel since time began. Knowledge — the knowledge that put cold-fusion power plants on all the Earth planets, in all the factories. New designs. New principles of mathematics and spatial mechanics. New methods, new ideas, much of it material Earth possibly might have discovered for itself in a thousand years, most of it material we never could have found unaided. And every bit of it was valid, every bit of it held out the promise of more once we had assimilated this incredible cargo.

When the survey ship *Luanae* reached the Earth Worlds, they say that the suspicion was thicker than anyone alive today could readily understand. They say they were going to court-martial the skipper for waiting all that time out there making up stories. And they say there was a powerful movement to suppress everything they brought back, out of fear that the new technology might in some way be a Trojan horse. But sheer cussed human curiosity got the better of all that, and though they started slowly, it wasn't too long before the Luanae devices and principles proved themselves out — spectacularly.

And in a few years, humanity was back again — in force. The main idea was to breach the Barrier — peaceably if possible, but breach it. Most of the ships, most of the men, did not make the attempt, so great was the impact of the Luanae truth and fellow feeling. Some did try, ramming, bombing, bringing up a hyper-magnetic generator ship to try warping the intangible structure of the Barrier. All failed; those who touched it died. Whenever that happened there was a great sound-less cry of mourning from the Luanae, but the Barrier remained.

When the survey ship discovered them, the Luanae had explained simply and clearly why the Barrier was there, and why it stayed. It seemed too simple a story, and buried as it was in such a mass of other data, it was overlooked or disbelieved. Mind you, that was before the Luanae had been recorded, before the human millions could 'hear' for themselves what a transmission from them was really like. Probably the Luanae realized this; at any rate, the story of the Barrier was the first Luanae recording to be widely distributed, and its impact was huge.

Such a simple story ... a people in some ways like humanity, perhaps a little swifter technologically, perhaps in some ways less demanding ... well, they lived a good deal longer, took a good deal less from the land to keep themselves alive. They had some things to be proud of – an art that can only be imagined outside the Barrier, and music of a kind. They did 'send' some of their literature, as you know ... ah. Then, they had a number of things to be ashamed of. Some wars, big ones. Three times they all but destroyed themselves, and climbed back up again. Then there was a long flowering, which seemed like something good, something fine. They developed a compassion, a philosophy of respect for the living and harmony with the laws of the universe – more than a religion, more than simply a way of life and thought. Through it, a good many things became unnecessary to them, and they forgot they had hands. ...

When they were attacked from space (this happened countless thousands of years ago) they could not defend themselves at all. They had forgotten the largest part of their fabulous technology; their machines were corroded, their skills had died, and worst of all, they had forgotten how to organize, how to be many men under one man's hand — for the duration. So they were enslaved.

They broke their chains at length — at some thirty thousand years' length. When they had driven out the invader, and followed him and destroyed him and all his worlds, they were a frightened and sober people. Their taste of quiet, or personal and individual fulfilment, was a touch of paradise to them and they deeply resented its loss. Their return to material power was in their minds a descent and a degradation. Yet they had learned a lesson and learned it well. They made up their minds to defend themselves in such a way that never again — positively, absolutely and forever — never again would they be attacked, no matter how long it might be, no matter how deep and distantly they buried their souls in their nameless, nebulous delights.

So after due consideration, they decided on the Barrier. They threw their total productivity — enormous, after their last war — and all their ingenuity into a defence to end all defences. They marked out a segment of the surrounding space, purposely enclosing ten times the volume which their computers specified as the most that they could conceivably ever need for themselves. They built a planetoid and stabilized it in an orbit around a dead sun not far from their cultural hub. This control planetoid, in ways as yet far too advanced for humanity to grasp, generated and maintained the Barrier itself. In addition, it gathered up cosmic debris and sucked it in, and with its mammoth automatic machinery, transmuted and smelted and cast and machined flight after flight of missiles — large and small. These were racked and stored by the hundreds of thousands, stationed throughout the Barrier-protected space in a myriad of automatically computed orbits. And so it was that anything which penetrated the Barrier, from any quarter, was instantly hunted down and killed.

There was some alarm at first over the fact that the Barrier, by its nature, must destroy anything leaving, as the missiles destroyed everything entering. But there seemed no valid answer to the question 'Why not?' The Luanae weren't going anywhere. They had space enough, and ten times space enough, for any roaming they chose to do. And they chose to do very little, for their orientation was back toward those golden years of introspection, of contemplative, inward self-realization, and their hunger for it was very great.

And so they locked the universe out, and themselves in –

And threw away the key.

The control planetoid was a machine – automatic, self-repairing; powered by cold fusion of two isotopes of hydrogen, and it could always get hydrogen. It made missiles and used them. When it used them, it gathered up the dust that was left and salvaged it and made more. When any outbound matter was destroyed by the inner surface of the Barrier, it gathered up the radiant energy of the pyre, and the ashes, and brought them in and used them. It was impregnable, inexhaustible, tireless and immortal. It brought safety, it brought peace.

It brought death to a nomad people, so vastly superior in intellect and in what has been translated from the Luanae 'sendings' as 'size-of-soul' that the Luanae, by that time steeped again in their unthinkable metaphysics, awoke to watch them approach, awe-struck, alive and aware of them. What they were can never now be known. Even the Luanae do not know. They say only that their thirty thousand years of slavery to the creatures who invaded them was but a scratch, a tow-stub, compared to the wound they suffered in the realization that they caused the destruction of these nameless nomads. The creatures swept down on the Barrier, unable to detect something unique in the universe, unwarned and unprepared, and were swallowed up by it. It is impossible to describe the impact of this event on the Luanae. Already deeply involved in their ancient philosophy, in tune with the universe and respecting all natural things: compassionate, life-reverent, humble and kind, they watched the destruction of their infinite superiors with an infinite horror. They realized then the extent of their folly, their crime in the creation of the Barrier. Already far gone again away from their technological peak, they again restored it. They surpassed it. They mobilized to pull down what they had put up, driven by guilt and horror at the thing they had done. It was the crucifixion of crucifixions, the murder of murders with the Messiah of Messiahs their irreplaceable victim.

And they failed. They had built too well. The planetoid destroyed everything that approached it. It was surrounded by miniature versions of the great Barrier, some turned inside out so that the disintegrating surface was encountered first. It picked apart, in a microsecond, everything they threw at it; ate it, digested it, and was nourished. The Luanae then undertook a frightening sacrifice, an appalling expense; in an effort to overload the planetoid's defences, they flung up thousands of missiles, ships, lumps of rock and debris, hurling it every which way between their stars and planets. Implacably the planetoid located the intrusive matter, compared it with its matrix of stored information on allowable bodies and their permitted circlings, and sought out and destroyed the offending ones, quite uncaring that many of them, tragically many, were manned. . . .

And in time they discovered that the planetoid was producing missiles and energy past its original capacity, consuming more than it had originally been designed to handle, computing more things more quickly. At that, they ceased to attack it, realizing belatedly that they had forced it to enlarge and strengthen itself — the only course open to a self-repairing machine stressed beyond its original endurance.

It was like Original Sin no longer a legend, but an experience and curse fully and presently upon them. They fell back then on the only thing left for them to do, as creatures of efficient conscience: they set up warnings.

They devised transmissions which covered the entire spectra of intelligence, transcending language, surpassing even symbolism. They set up automatic beacons to radiate the warning in all directions, each beam overlapping the next. Bitterly, they organized a trade of monitors to watch over the automatic machines, which they never again would trust. The monitors were ritualized like a priesthood, drilled like slave-legions, marinated in the impulses of duty. Once that was done and tested past any conceivable fault or failure, they settled to a new level of life, neither blindly mechanical, like that which had produced the planefoid, nor vegetative and contemplative, like that which had left them open to slavery, but a middle ground, based on the ancient convictions of respect for life and its ways in the rigid and marvellous frame of the universe; and implemented by an unrusting technology.

So it was that the Luanae were at last in a position to make their greatest and most mature discovery — a thing known to each of them as individuals, but until now unrealized in terms of life-groups. A man cannot exist alone. He must be a member of something, a piece, an integer of some larger whole. Men plus men make cities, which band together to form states, then countries, then worlds; and never can a sole unit exist alone and unsupplied. Communication and intercourse are necessary and vital; without them the lone unit is a brief accident unnoticed by the universe and forever forgotten. So, behind their gigantic ghastly barricade, the Luanae at last acknowledged membership in a grouping greater than species, and declared themselves belonging to Life and dedicated to the survival of its total membership.

This, then, was the self-imprisoned people discovered by an Earth scoutship, in the business of locating terrestrial planets for humanity. The Luanae rose with a shout at the sight of them. This was Life — life to aid and life to share. For until Earth came to them they saw themselves dying like a surrounded city, like a lone traveller, like an amputated limb, like any other life separated from its sustaining body. Earth brought life to the Luanae, and the Luanae enlisted themselves in Earth's search for life.

A lousy trip. A suicide trip, with a skipper and utility monkey horse-blindered by their duties, three crackpots and an unemployed and unusable CG. And me, Palmer, with what could be the answer. I had faith in it; I liked its math. I had little or no hope that it would be tried — really tried full-scale, and done right. People don't know enough. They don't think really straight. They turn the wrong valves and push the wrong buttons. Palmer should have a thousand hands and the ability to be simultaneously in a thousand places. Then this business of being the wasp-waist in the history of Life and the Lives of the two cultures — this would make more sense. I shall be bungled out of history, I told myself as we ground along in the nothingness of subspace — the Luanae subspace, given us by Luanae cold-fusion generators. I'm coming, I'm coming, I told the Luanae silently, but I bring the enemy; I bring bungling; and, my marvels, you'll succumb to stupidity as will I, for it's the last and mightiest enemy of them all, against which you and I may not prevail.

114

I watched Potter picking away, and I silently bore Donato's cough, and I gave my approval to big-eared England because he had so little to say to anybody; I tried to remember what exactly it was that made Nils Blum the utility-monkey funny to me when I saw him first; I hoped to recapture it and laugh again, but I never made it. I swore sometimes at Donato's eternal helpfulness and I ignored the skipper, because who wants to talk all the screaming time about ship's business and the business of ships gone by? ... I said nothing where the CG could hear me, and tightened up in painful empathy when I saw one or another of the ship's company floundering and defending and doubting when she repeated his words. I did nothing about any of these annoyances, except maybe the time I suggested to the skipper that he feed the CG at times other than our mess, so I didn't have to witness her purposeless wreckage of even the little things men believe in. He bought that, and it had a double advantage. We not only were spared the sight of her at meals, but she took to spending her time aft in the 'monkey's cage' among the mops and drums of cleaning aerosol and sewer-line scrapers. If Nils Blum objected, then monkeylike he could pass it off by scratching and chewing a straw. I came through there once and saw them sitting across from each other at Blum's little table, elbows almost touching, not speaking and not looking at each other. And by the Lord she was crying, and I must say it did me good. I had a mind to go ask the monkey how he managed it, but I don't involve myself with the un-skilled.

We got where we were going and snapped out of the nothing into the something. We took a bearing on the Luanae galaxy and it was quite a sight, a long irregular sausage of an island galaxy, with its unmistakable signpost, the long regular black swath of the Barrier's edge where it impinged on, and shut out, the rest of the bodies in the formation. We ducked under again for half an hour and came up again too close to see the swath, but close enough at last to get the Luanae greeting.

That I can't tell you about.

Captain Steev piped us all into the messhall in mid-morning, which would have annoyed me if I could think of anything I'd rather be doing — but there just wasn't anything to do, or to want to do, instead. So I shuffled in with the rest of them — Potter, England, Donato. Blum and the CG were back with the mops, I imagine. The captain let us all be seated and stood at the end of the table and knocked on a coffee mug self-consciously. He said:

'Gentlemen. We have as you know arrived at our site of operations. We have among the four of you four different specialists with, as I understand it, four new and as yet untried attacks on the problem of penetrating the Luanae Barrier. I need not,' he said, and then went right on as if he needed to anyway, '. . . need not tell you of the vital importance of this task. The entire history of humanity might — not might, *does* — depend on it. If you, or men like you, fail to solve this problem soon, we can expect our entire civilization to explode, like a dying sun, through the internal pressures of its own contracting mass.' He coughed to cover up the floridity of his phrasing, and little Donato happily joined in. I saw one of England's wide flat hands move on the table, to cover the other and hold it down.

'Now then,' said the captain. He bent from the waist and removed his hand from his side pocket. In it was a sleek little remote mike. 'This is for the record, gentlemen. You first, I think, Mr. Palmer?'

'Me first what?' I wanted to know.

'Your plan, sir. Your approach, attack, whatever it pleases you to call it. Your projected method of cracking the Barrier.'

I looked around at what passed for an audience, coughing, picking, glowering wetly. I said, 'In the first place, my plan has been fully detailed and filed with the proper authorities — men who are in a position to understand my specialty. I believe that copies of these papers are on file with you. I suggest that you look at them and save us both the trouble.'

'I'm afraid you don't understand,' said the captain, looking flustered. He gestured at the mike. 'This is for the record. I've got to have the oral rundown. It's . . . it's . . . well, for the record.'

'Then I say to the recording, for the record,' I barked, right into the mike, 'that I am not accustomed to being asked to make speeches before a lay audience, which cannot be expected to understand one word in ten of what I have to say. And I refer the recording and its auditors, whoever they may be, to the files in which my detailed report is presented, for proof not only of my project but of the fact that these assembled, and no doubt those listening to this record, would in all likelihood not know what I was talking about.' I glared up at the captain. 'Does that satisfy the record, Lieutenant?'

'Captain,' corrected the captain mildly. 'Really.'

'A mistake,' I allowed. 'I never make mistakes accidentally, you understand.' I waved at the mike. 'Let's let the record stand with that, d'you mind?'

'Mr. Potter,' said the captain, and I leaned back, pleased with myself.

Potter removed his finger and immediately replaced it. 'Well I don't bind tellig you bine,' he said nasally. 'I'm in field bechanics, as you dough. I have bade certain calculations which indicate that the stresses present in the barrier skin are subject on bobentary distortion under the stress of sball area, high intenstidty focussed bagnetic fields of about one hudred billion gauss per square centimetre at focuss. That's *billion*,' he amended. 'Not *billion*.'

117

I wondered how the record would make out the difference.

'Very good, very good, Mr. Potter,' said the captain. 'Unless I am mistaken, you propose to breach the Barrier momentarily with a high-intensity focussed magnetic field. Is that correct?'

Potter nodded, a gesture which carried through his right wrist.

'Very well,' said the captain. I blew out disgustedly through my nostrils, looking at Potter. His business was as disgusting as his hobby. If I knew as little about my specialty as he did about his, I'd never get trapped into talking about it.

'Mr. Donato?'

'Yes, Captain Steev, yes sir!' Donato cried, all blushes and eagerness. 'Well, sir, I'm in ballistics. What I propose is a two-part missile aimed to graze the Barrier in such a way that at the moment of contact, it separates, one segment glancing back outside, the other entering and proceeding inward. This is on the theory that although the control planetoid reacts instantaneously, its sensors report only one event at one locality at a given moment. I feel I have a fifty-fifty chance, then, of slipping one part through while the other part is being reported grazed and gone. I think a minimum of one hundred thirty shots, fired in four groups and at four slightly different approach angles, would establish whether or not the theory is tenable.'

'Tenable?' I gasped. 'Why, you — you nincompoop!' That's the first time in my entire life I ever called anyone that, but as I looked at him, blushing and grinning and wanting to do right, there just wasn't another applicable term. 'What makes you think —'

'Mr. England?' said the skipper, much louder than I have ever heard him speak before. I confess I was startled. Before I could quite recover myself, England answered.

118

'In the area of mis,' he said in a whispery voice which at that point failed him. He swallowed with all his might and then made a weak flickery smile. 'In the field of missiles, my chief concern is first, a series of tests to determine the exact nature of the internal control pulses in the hunting missiles, the frequency and wave-height of the command pulses in the guided missiles, with a view to jamming or redirecting them. Second, I plan to lob some solids through the barrier at low velocities in order to study the metallurgical content of the missiles, with a view to the design of sensing-dodging equipment, and possibly some type of repulsion field, designed to force the missiles into a near miss.'

'Very succinct,' said the captain, and I wondered how he knew what was succinct or not about a specialty. 'Now that we've got the swing of this little discussion, perhaps, Mr. Palmer, you would like to reconsider and join it.'

'Perhaps I would at that,' I said, stopping to think it over. After all, a little sense ought to be added to this exhibition of maundering incompetence, if only for balance. 'Then if you must know, the only tenable method of approaching the problem lies in the area of explosive stress. No one but myself seems to have noticed the almost perfectly spherical shape of the Barrier. A sphere in any flexing material is a certain indication of some dynamic tension, a container and the contained in equilibrium, with the analog of some fluid differential like the air inside and outside an inflated balloon. You don't follow me.'

'Go on,' said the captain, holding his head as if he was listening.

'Why, all it will take is a toroidal mass equipped with a subspace generator and an alternator. If this is placed upon the Barrier margin and caused to vibrate into and out of the subspace state, there will be a portion of the Barrier — that which is surrounded by the toroid —

119

which will be included in the vibration. The effect then is in causing a circular section of the Barrier to be in nonexistence for part of the time. It is my conclusion that this small breach will cause the Barrier to collapse like that toy balloon I mentioned. Q.E.D. Lieutenant.' I leaned back.

'Captain,' said the captain tiredly. Then he looked me in the eye and said, 'I regret to inform you, Mr. Palmer, that you are completely wrong. Blum!' he bellowed suddenly, 'coffee out here!'

'Hah!' came the monkey's voice. It was as near as he ever let himself get to aye-aye sir. He must have had the tray ready before the skipper called, because he came out with it loaded and steaming. He set it down in the middle of the table and retired to a corner. At the side of my eye, I saw the CG sidle out of the 'cage' and go to stand silently beside him. But I wasn't in a mood for anything but this preposterous allegation from the captain. I got to my feet so I could look down at him. 'Did I understand you to say,' I ground out, cold as Neptune, 'that in *your* opinion *I* am wrong?'

'Quite wrong. The Barrier is a position, an infinite locus, not a material substance, and is therefore not subject to the laws and treatments of matter per se.'

I have been known to splutter when I am angry unless I try not to. I found myself trying very hard not to. 'I have reduced every observation on that surface known to man,' I informed him, 'to mathematical symbology, and from it have written a consecutive sequence of occasions which proves beyond doubt that the surface is as I say and will act as I say. You seem to forget that this is on the record, admiral, and this may mean you are making a permanent rather than a temporary fool of yourself.' I sat down, feeling better.

'Captain,' said the captain wearily. He turned and took a paper from the stack of folders which I noticed for the first time lay there. He flashed it; at first glance it looked like a page of figures over which a child had superimposed a crude and scratchy picture of a Christmas tree in red. He said, 'Equation number one-three-two, four pi sigma over theta plus the square root of four pi sigma quantity squared.' I could not help noticing that as he reeled it off, he was waving the paper, not reading from it.

I said, 'I recognize the equation. Well?'

'Well, nothing,' snapped the captain. 'Unwell, I'd call it. Heh.' He slid the sheet over to me. 'If you will observe, to be consistent with the preceding series, the integer sigma is not whole but factorial, in view of which an increasing error is introduced wherein — but see for yourself.'

I looked. What looked like a crude picture of a Christmas tree was the correction, in red, of the symbol he had mentioned, and the scrawled figures of three corrected factors in the next equation and seven in the third following, until the red marks became a whole line. I said. 'Might I ask who has had the effrontery to scribble all over these calculations?'

'Oh, I did,' said the captain. 'I thought it might be a good idea to rework the whole series, just in case, and I'm glad I did. You ought to be too.'

I looked again at the sheet and swallowed sand. A man has to major for a considerable time in some highly creative math to be able to do what had been done here. A thing or two came to my lips but I would not say them, because they were for my figures and against his, yet it could not be denied that his were right. To save something out of this, I growled at him, 'I think, sir, you owe me an explanation as to why you have chosen publicly to humiliate me.'

'I didn't humiliate you. Those figures humiliated you, and they're your figures,' he said, and shrugged. I glanced at Potter and England. They were grinning broadly. I looked up suddenly and caught the flat grey stare of the CG. 'They're your figures,' she murmured, and anyone hearing her would swear she knew for certain that I had copied them from somebody else's work. There was such a flame of insistence burning up in me that they were *so* my figures, that I could barely contain it. But contain it I did; they were not figures I was anxious to claim at the moment. I was very confused. I slumped down in my chair.

'You're next, Mr. Potter. I'm sorry to have to inform you that although in theory the Barrier does yield under the stress of a magnetic field such as you describe, it would take a generator somewhat larger than this ship to supply it; the affected area would be just about what you said – a square centimetre; and finally, it wouldn't be a hole in the Barrier, but what you might call a replacement patch. In other words, the affected area will, when surrounded by the so-called Barrier skin, act precisely like part of that skin in all respects.'

Potter put his hobby finger out for inspection and was so distressed he forgot to look at it. 'Are ... are you sure?'

'That's what happened the last seven times it was tried.'

Potter made a wordless thing, a sort of moan, or sigh. I did not feel like grinning at him as he had at me. England did not grin either, because I think he realized what was coming. He just sat there wondering just how it would come.

It came at Donato first. 'Mr. Donato –'

'Yes, *sir*, cap'n.'

'You propose a two-piece missile. You seem to forget, as many another has before you, that the Barrier offers no resistance to penetration and therefore needs no complicated hanky-panky to get something inside. In addition, it's unimportant whether or not an object is sensed by the skin and reported to control, or whether it's picked up a minute or an hour later by one of the

122

hunting missiles. You've attacked the whole problem with a view to getting something inside, which isn't a problem, and overlooked what to do once you're inside, which is.'

'Oh cap'n, I'm sorry,' said Donato, sticken. He burst into a sharp series of barking coughs. There were tears in his eyes. 'Oh, I'm sorry. I'm sorry.'

'Nothing to be sorry about,' said the captain. 'Got it yet, Mr. England?'

'Whuh? Oh,' said the missile expert. 'I guess I was off base about the jamming. Suddenly it seems to me that's so obvious it must have been tried and it doesn't work.'

'Right, it doesn't. That's because the frequency and amplitude of the control pulses make like purest noise — they're genuinely random. So trying to jam them is like trying to jam FM with an AM signal. You hit it so seldom you might as well not try.'

'What do you mean, random? You can't control anything with random noise.'

The captain thumbed over his shoulder at the Luanae galaxy. 'They can. There's a synchronous generator in the missiles that reproduces the *same random noise*, peak by pulse. Once you do that, modulation's no problem. I don't know *how* they do it. They just do. The Luanae can't explain it; the planetoid developed it.'

England put his head down almost to the table. 'The same random,' he whispered from the very edge of sanity.

As if anxious to push him the rest of the way, the captain said cheerfully. 'Good thinking on that proposal to study the metal content of the missiles. Only there isn't any. They're a hundred percent dielectric synthetics, God knows exactly what. The planetoid can transmute, you know. What little circuitry the missiles have is laid out in fluid-filled pipes, capillary coils, things like that. There seems to be some sort of instantaneous transition from solid to liquid and back. The

123

liquid conductors are solid dielectrics again just as soon as they have passed whatever current they're supposed to pass, and that's done in microseconds.'

'Radar transparent,' concluded England dolefully.

'For all practical purposes,' agreed the captain. 'Well, that seems to be that, gentlemen.'

'Just you tell me one thing,' I said before I could stop myself. 'Precisely what in hell are we doing here at all?'

'Precisely what you came to do,' said the captain. He picked up his folders. 'Blum,' he said, 'I sense that these four gentlemen might be happier without an audience, even you.'

'Come on, Virginia.'

The captain started out forward and the monkey and the CG headed aft. We all sat where we were. After a time England said, 'Why didn't he tell me he knew so much about missiles?'

'Did you ask him?' snapped Potter.

That was the question and answer I had been humbly formulating too. I said, 'What did he mean, we are here to do what we came to do?'

'Maybe he wants us to get oriented, is all,' said Donato sheepishly. 'Get off theory, you know. Like field work. On the spot.'

'If he thinks he's jolting my inspiration, he's crazy,' gloomed England. He wiped his wet eyes with the backs of his hands, leaving them still wet. 'The jolt I got. The inspiration I can't find.'

'He should have told us before, right at the start. Maybe by now we'd have a whole new set of figures.' He caught my sharp look and immediately said, 'Theorems, I mean, friend, I didn't mean to say figures.' Somehow that didn't help. 'Get out of here, Donato,' I said.

'Sure, friend, sure,' he said and got out like always, smiling. He went into his room and closed the door. We could hear him coughing.

'Like a box you have in your room ten years,' Potter

124

was muttering, 'it all of a sudden goes boing and there's a jumpid-jack.' I was going to ask him what he was talking about and then realized he was talking about the captain. I saw his point. Why *hadn't* he called this meeting weeks ago? 'He must like things to look futile,' I said. 'I'm going back to bed.'

'Be too,' said Potter. I got up. Potter and England stayed where they were. They were going to talk about me.

I just didn't care.

I dreamed I was walking in a meadow smelling the sweet fresh odour of snowdrops, when all of a sudden they grew taller and taller, or I grew smaller and smaller, and I saw that instead of stems, the snowdrops were growing on a sequence of equations. I began to read them off, but they got all twisted and jumbled and started to grab at my feet. I fell and grunted and caught hard at the edges of the bunk and was totally awake. I turned over and looked at the overhead. I felt clear-headed but lethargic. I thought I could still smell the snowdrops.

Then I noticed the whine. It was far away, but persistent. The lights looked funny. They seemed to be flickering slightly, but when you looked straight at them, they were steady. I didn't like it. It made me feel dizzy.

I got up and went out into the corridor. Nobody was around. Then a timid voice said behind me, 'Virginia in there?'

I jumped and turned. It was the monkey, cringing against the bulkhead. 'Gee *god*!' I answered him in disgust, but as I turned away he leaned forward and peered into my room anyway.

I went into the messhall and knocked on the decanter and when it steamed, poured coffee. Somewhere in the background I heard a wistful murmur, and then Potter's shocked voice: 'In *here*? Monkey, didn't they tell you? I like *girls*.' In a moment he came shuffling in and headed for the coffee. 'What time is it, Palmer?'

I shrugged. I looked at the clock but it didn't seem to make any sense to me. 'God,' said Potter, and sniffed noisily. 'I feel all ... disconnected. I got a buzzing in my ears. My eyes – it's sort of flickery.'

I looked at him curiously, wondering what it must be like to be a man who so readily relates everything around him to himself. 'That isn't your flicker, it's ours. The buzz too, though I'd call it a sort of whine.'

He looked very relieved. 'You hear it too. What happens here, anyway?'

I drank some coffee and looked at the clock again. 'What's the matter with that clock?' I demanded.

Potter craned to look at it. 'Can't be. Can't be.'

Donato came in, his face scrubbed and shining. 'Morning, Palmer. Potter. Well, I wondered which one of us would fall first, and I guess I know now, and who'd a' thunk it.' He nodded aft and began coughing. We looked. The monkey was stepping off one foot and on to the other in front of England's door.

'You ought to mind your own business, Don.'

'Oh sure,' said Donato agreeably. 'Guess you're right at that.' Just then England flung his door open, saw Nils Blum crouching there, and recoiled with an odd high squeak. Immediately he growled, in his deepest bass, 'Don't hang around me, monk,' and pushed past the utility man without a backward glance. We watched, looking past him as he approached. Blum ducked his head inside England's door, withdrew it, took a step toward us and stopped, his jaw working silently, his big wrinkled head held a little askew.

'But hungry, I'm hungry,' said England. 'Whatever time is it?'

'Clock's busted,' said Potter, and suddenly laughed. We all looked at him. 'Well,' he said, pointing at England, 'it's not him either.'

126

'You were just saying to Don, he ought to mind his own business,' I snapped. I wonder, I thought to myself, if he knows I cut at him because he picks his nose?

'What business? What goes?' England demanded.

'By holy creepin' Kramden,' said Donato to himself. He looked aft at the miserable figure there and forward at the closed door to the wardroom and control. 'What do you know.'

'He is a very surprising man,' I said.

'Who? Who? The skipper? What's he done now?' England demanded.

'Virginia seems to be missing,' Donato said.

Hearing her name, Blum ran three steps toward us and then stopped in the messhall door, looking timidly at our faces, one by one. 'Well,' said Potter, 'rank has its privileges.'

England blew sharply through his nostrils, expressing a great deal and disposing of the matter. He glanced at the clock. 'What'd you say is wrong with it?'

'Nothing's wrong with it.' We turned abruptly and faced the captain. There was an oddness about him, a set to his jaw, a certain hard something in his eye, that hadn't been there at all before. Or maybe it had, there at the table this morning. (Was that this morning? What the clock said just made no sense at all.) I looked at the captain and past him, through his open door, through the wardroom with his neat bunk at the side, on forward to the control console and observation blister.

There wasn't anybody up there.

From the other doorway, the utility monkey whispered, 'Sir?'

'Something the matter with the lights, captain,' Donato said.

'It's all right,' said the captain shortly. He went to the messhall peeper and switched it on. He dialled for starboard view and stepped back.

We crowded around it. Everything looked about the

same out there, the wide vein of jewels straggling across the sky, then the unrelieved black.

'Show you something,' said the captain. He moved the controls, and the view zoomed in toward the stars. At close to peak magnification, he switched to the fine tuning and got the crosshairs where he wanted them. 'Know what that is?'

It was a ball, shiny, golden. It was impossible to say how big. Then I heard England gasp.

'I've seen that before. Pictures. That's the Barrier Control – the planetoid!'

'So close?'

'Just because the Barrier is a sphere,' said the captain, 'everyone assumes the control has to be in the centre. Well, it isn't. It's right here at the edge, and heaven help anything that goes in there in a rush, trying to converge on the centre!'

'Sir . . .' came the whisper.

'Now look,' said the captain, winding the zoom handle again. The view backed away from the golden sphere until it was almost lost. Suddenly the screen filled with a flat-topped, streamlined . . .

'A pod, a ship's pod!' said England.

The captain stepped back a pace and watched the pod with glowing eyes. His hands were pressed tight together, and some great suppressed excitement yearned in him to burst free. We looked from him to the peeper. Under his breath, the captain said, 'Git'm. Go git'm!'

'Sir. . . .'

'Shut up, monk.'

'That pod's inside the Barrier!' somebody said. Me, I think.

'Look, look there!'

It was like a segment of ivory knitting needle. It was turning slowly end over end. It approached the pod slowly, high, passed close by and drifted out of the picture.

128

'A missile, a big one. My God, what's happened?'

'The Barrier's down,' said the captain as if he couldn't hold the words inside any longer. 'It's down, you see? It's gone, and the missiles all dead.'

'Sir, oh cap'n ... I can't find Virginia. Where's Virginia, cap'n?'

'You're looking at her, Blum. You're looking right at her,' said the captain, his eyes fixed on the screen.

Something hit us, scattered us. For a moment the messhall was a swirl of grunts and outraged yells, and then the utility monkey had tumbled us aside and was standing in front of the peeper, one hand on each side frame. He seemed a half a head taller, all at once, and his one hairy arm, where it passed close by me, had cords on it I hadn't known about before; his head was a lion's head.

Suddenly he barked, 'What'd you do? What'd you do?' He was talking to the captain, who kept looking over Blum's shoulder at the picture, and he was laughing softly. Then the monkey whirled from the screen, turning as if to turn was to tear something, and he faced the captain and said again, 'What'd you do? What'd you do with Virginia?'

The captain stopped laughing altogether and was a captain duty-talking to a utility monkey. 'I gave her her orders and I put her in that pod and sent her on her way. Any objections, mister?'

Blum's eyes began to protrude, honestly, you could see them press outward. His mouth opened slowly, slowly, and a wetness suddenly scored the corner of the mouth and down the side of the chin; the hands came up, clawed, half-grasping. The nostrils trembled, trembled ... and then he screamed, so loud, so close to us, it was like a big light flashing to blind us; we reared back from that scream, pawing at it. Next thing was Blum, crouched over and peering ahead as he ran, trying to go somewhere, not knowing how; he ran

129

crazily to the airlock hatch and hit it with his fists, and turned with his back to it and screamed again. 'You send me, you hear? You send me with Virginia, you hear me, cap'n?'

Donato strolled over toward him and smiling, said the stupidest thing I ever heard squirted into a violent silence: 'Aw come on, monkey, let's all be chums.' Blum screamed again and Donato didn't wait to get turned around, he ran straight backwards until he hit me, and I caught him and held him up so he didn't fall. 'Cap'n, sir,' Donato said, squinching his head around as he dangled from my hands, 'he won't mind me at all, cap'n.'

'Get to your quarters, Blum,' said the captain from way back in his throat.

'You bring her back, or you send me out with her,' slavered Blum. 'You hear me?'

'Get . . . to . . . your . . . quarters.'

Blum put up his claws. He began walking toward the captain, chewing on his own mouthparts and his eyes were crazy. The captain bent a little low and put his arms out a little from his sides, and moved very slowly toward Blum. We all got back out of the way.

Blum said, 'Now, you hear me?' very softly, and leaped. The captain stepped aside and hit him, I thought it was on the head but England told me later it was on the side of the neck, toward the back. The monkey was in midair when the captain hit him, and he went right down on the deck on his face, and he didn't put out his hands to stop himself, and he didn't move.

We all looked at him and then at each other.

'Take him to his quarters,' said the captain. His voice startled me because it wasn't where I thought it was, standing by the sprawled-out monkey. He was already across the room staring into the peeper; for him the thing was finished, probably his heart wasn't quick any

130

more; he was back with his work, his job. The rest of us had poundings in the side of our necks and we didn't know what to do.

'Go on, go on. Get him out of here. You, Palmer. You're the biggest.'

I was going to splutter but I held on tight to it and didn't. I said, 'See here, I don't have to —'

From back in his throat like before, he spoke to me. It was a different thing being the one he spoke to like that and not watching somebody else get it. He said, '*You* see here, you do have to. Whatever I say, you have to, not only you, Palmer, but all four of you clowns. The part's over and the work's done, and from now on out you mind me and think first of what I want. At all times. Is that clear, mister?'

I said, loud, 'Well, I —' and the skipper ripped his eyes away from the screen, almost like Blum, tearing something, and looked at me. So I picked up the monkey's shoulders and dragged him back to his cabin. It was just like ours only he didn't have quite so much stuff lying around, or anyway what there was was in square stacks. I tumbled him on to the bunk and closed the door, because that was the only clear place to lean back against, and I leaned back on it and tried to get my breath back.

The monkey started to make a scratchy sound in the back of his throat. I looked down at him. His head was twisted to one side. It was jammed against the pillow. His eyes were open. 'Cut that out, monk.' He went right on doing it. 'That noise, cut it out, hear me? I said, you hear me, mister?' That 'mister' didn't sound a bit like the skipper's. I was embarrassed.

The monkey's eyes stayed open and I realized he wasn't blinking them, he wasn't seeing out of them. I couldn't stand that breathing noise so finally I straightened out his head and put the pillow under it. He stopped the noise right away. He closed his eyes.

131

I still couldn't get my breath. He had blood on his face; maybe that was it.

He didn't open his eyes but he began to talk, very fast, very soft. It was like being too far away from someone to understand what was being said, and then it was like coming closer. . . . '. . . all she had to do was let herself and she couldn't do it, she couldn't just stop fighting and believe. It was like she'd die if she believed anything. She wanted to. More than anything she wanted to. But it was like someone told her, if you believe in anything you'll die.' He opened his eyes suddenly and saw me and closed them again. 'Palmer. You Palmer you, you saw it your own self, the time she cried. All that time, all those weeks, those grey eyes still and hiding whatever it was she had inside her, and me begging her and begging: Virginia, oh Virginia, I don't care what you think of me, I wouldn't want you to love me, Virginia. But only believe me; you can so be loved, you're worth loving, I love you. I do, Virginia; just you believe that once, because it's true, and after that you'll be able to believe other things . . . little ones at first; I'll help you with them, and always tell you the truth. I said, don't love me, Virginia, or think about it at all. I wouldn't know what to do with it if you gave me anything like that. I said, just trust me is all I want, so you can ask me what's the truth and I'll tell you. But believe I love you: I'm not much, Virginia, so I guess that's not too much to start on. Believe I love you, Virginia, will you just do that? And she . . .'

He lay with his eyes open for a long time and I thought he was unconscious again, but then he blinked his eyes and went on, '. . . she cried, all at once, all over, and she said, "Monkey, monkey, you're tearing me up, can't you see? I want to believe you. I want to believe you more than anything in the world. But I can't, I don't know how, I'm not supposed to, I'm not allowed." That's what she said. And she cried again and said,

"But I want to believe you, monkey. You just don't know how much I want to believe that. Only . . . nothing is what it looks like, nothing is what it's supposed to be, no one really wants what they say they want. I can't believe them and I can't believe you. Suppose I believed you and then the day came when things were all straight and true, and they let you see everything; and suppose I found out then that everything you said wasn't so; found out maybe there was no you at all, monkey. What about that? I couldn't stand that, I don't dare," she said, "I don't dare believe you, because I want to. If I don't believe anything about anything or anyone, then if things get all true I can start there and be all right without losing anything." And she cried some more and then, you, Palmer, you came in, and in a second she was back inside her flat grey eyes. So she didn't believe me and that's why.'

I couldn't get my breath. Blum couldn't get his breath. I leaned on the door and he lay on the bed and we panted.

'There was a difference,' he whispered, chasing some thought he was having. 'She had a way of making you doubt anything you said. I told her my mother could cook. She said, "Your mother could cook" in that slow way, and you know, I had to think and wonder if my mother really could. That's what I mean. But I said to her, Virginia, you know, I love you, and she said, "You love me" in that same way, like who ever heard of such a thing; but what I'm trying to say, that didn't touch me, when she did that when I said I love you. I looked into how I felt and I felt the same no matter what she said. So about that, there was a difference. That's how it was all right to say believe me, believe me about that. I knew that things could change, I knew that almost anything I told her could be wrong, some way. But not that. She could trust me with that. And she wanted to. At least I got that.'

I leaned against the door feeling embarrassed and then I could turn it to anger. I said, 'You're stupid, monkey, you know? You're crew, she's CG. She couldn't stop you. Why didn't you just go right ahead? That's what she's aboard for.'

But that didn't make him angry. He looked up at the ceiling and said quietly, 'Yeah, she said that too. She said, you don't know what you want, monkey, she said. She said, this is what you want. So go ahead, only stop talking about, you know. I said no. I said there could be a time but I hadn't thought about it yet; I wanted something else first, I wanted her to believe me. She said I was crazy and to keep away from her then, but after, you saw it, Palmer. After, she said she wanted to believe me, more than anything.' He was quiet at last, breathing easily, thinking about something to smile at. I spoke to him but he didn't answer. He was asleep, I guess. I opened the door quietly and closed it on him and went back to the messhall.

They were all there by the peeper, watching. I said, 'He's asleep now but there's going to be particular hell to pay when he wakes up and really understands she isn't here.'

The skipper looked away from the screen at me and back again. He wouldn't spit on the messhall deck, but he might as well, the way his face looked. He couldn't worry about that monkey.

I said to Potter, 'What happens?'

Potter said, 'Whether to get mad or glad, I don't know. You specialist you, Palmer, you're a clown. And England. Donato. Me too. Virginia, she was the specialist all along. She was the one this whole thing is for. How much farther?' he called out.

'A few metres,' said Donato, absorbed. I looked at the peeper. The ship's pod, that long false underbelly we'd hauled all the way from the Earth planets, it was drifting in close to that golden ball. That ball, I could see

134

now, it was big as a supership if you could roll a supership into a ball. It was big as some moons. There were pale sticks drifting all over, dozens of them. 'Dead missiles, you see?' said Potter, watching the screen. 'All dead. Every single cold-fusion power plant and explosive in a thousand kilometres is dead. Maybe more. Ours too.'

'Ours?'

'That hum, that flicker. We're not tapping a cold-fusion plant now, Palmer. We're taking off a steam turbine, water superheated by a paraboilic mirror from that sun yonder.'

'Steam turbine take us home?'

'Stupid!'

Donato chimed in. It was weird. Everybody talking whispery, as if loud noises would spoil something in the peeper. Nobody looked at anybody to talk, just kept watching the peeper, some of them moving the mouth all to one side to talk to one, to the other side to talk to someone else. Donato said, 'Little turbine wouldn't move this can half a length.'

England said, 'It's all right. What she's doing, she's going in there to leech on to that planetoid. First there's a catalyst that will crumble a pit in the armour, because a bomb'll hardly scratch it. Then when the skin's thin enough, she's got a bomb there. It goes off, and no more Barrier.'

'He said the Barrier's gone.'

'Sure. She damped it. She's holding it dead. If she let go, bango, back comes the Barrier and all those missiles come to life.'

'What's this damped, holding it dead, letting go — what is all this?' I was getting impatient.

The skipper saw fit to say something. 'We call it the D-field because . . .' He was quite a long time. He said, 'Because that way it sounds like something we know about, can know about.' He flicked a quick glance at all

135

of us, as if somebody was going to laugh. Nobody was going to laugh. 'What it is,' said the skipper, hating to say it, 'it's doubt. I mean – well, doubt, that's all.'

Nobody said anything. Doubt, all right. But doubt has a way of getting invisible after a captain makes all those loud captain noises like he did.

I imagine he knew that. None of it was our business, not any more, but he didn't want to be doubted, not even by us ... clowns. He said, 'What we did, we found Virginia trying to commit suicide. She had this doubt thing on her back, naturally. She didn't want to go on, because she had nothing she could believe in. Or just plain believe. Well, we took her and gave her some treatments ... I'm a skipper, I don't know the details ... anyway, she came out of it with what she had when she went in, but more so. Much more. You all felt it – don't tell me you didn't. She could make a man doubt his own name.'

I said 'Yeah,' only realizing when I heard it that I'd said it aloud.

Captain Steev watched the screen for a while and said under his breath, 'That's right ... that's a girl. ...' And then to us: 'It was a cute problem. Given that a concentrated disbelief in things could have an effect like this – just for the sake of argument – if you want someone to stop a big power plant from a great distance with this faculty, how do you transport that someone in a ship powered with the same type of plant?'

'If it was a machine, now,' said England, 'I'd say assemble it only when you wanted to use it.'

'That's the way they did with the first fission bombs,' said Donato knowledgeably. 'They didn't put it together until it was due to blow. They blew it *by* putting it together. But ... a person, now. ...'

'You've got the idea. You can disbelieve in anything until you know what it is, or at least what people think it is. I can't believe or disbelieve that *pyoop* is the word for

136

godmother in High Martian. I just don't know. Well — Virginia didn't know one way or another about a cold-fusion plant, though I swear ours gasped a time or two on the way out. She has a large charge of it.'

England said with sudden impatience, 'Excuse me, cap'n, but the only reason I can stand here talking about this is I see it working.'

'Let me tell you, then. The cold-fusion plant is a Luanae idea. It's real simple-minded. Anybody can understand it once it's explained to them. Everything was set up when we came out here, including you four. The crackpot experts. The wide-eyed hobbyists who knew more than people who've been in this all their lives. But far as she was concerned, you were experts right up to the time I set you up and knocked you down, factorial sigma and the square-centimetre magnetic field, hah! She doubted you were experts when she first saw you, just because she doubted everything. When she saw what I did to you, she felt she was right to doubt. She reached a . . . sort of peak disbelief. My God, didn't you feel it? . . . look there, she's leeched down. Now the catalyst will be working on the armour. It won't be long now.'

'I still don't see how just plain disbelief can shut down power plants.'

'Not power plants. Just cold-fusion plants. Well, let me tell you and you'll understand. I put a shot of sleep-gas in your ventilators and got you all out of the way. Then —'

'Snowdrops,' I said, remembering.

'Then I put her in the pod and told her to ride it, that's all. Except I . . . armed her . . . like you arm a bomb, you see? I told her what a cold-fusion plant is. She didn't care one way or the other, mind, but she listened while I explained it to her, all the parts. Then I gave her a paper and told her this is exactly what happens. I told her to read it as soon as the red light on the panel went on, which would be when she was clear of the ship.'

'Read what?' somebody asked, after it got too quiet. It was a long wait, watching that pod leeched to the planetoid and nothing happening but white sticks drifting, rocks, bits of stuff the planetoid had pulled in but hadn't been able to eat. . . .

'The cold-fusion formula, that's all. Written out in words of one cylinder. When Hydrogen One and Hydrogen Two are in the presence of mu mesons, they fuse into Helium Three with an energy yield in electron volts of 5.4 times ten to the fifth power. That's what was on the paper. She knew, piece by each, what the parts were – what mu mesons and Helium 3 are and what is meant by that many electron volts. She had all that buried deep in her before we left the Earth Planets. She'd had no occasion to put them together, that's all. And here I come saying (on paper), "This gadget does exactly such and such." Well, she just out-and-out doesn't believe it. That would make no never mind to a turbine or a power drill, but when you get into sub-atomic particles, clouds of them, involved in a catalysis – untouched in the long run, but I imagine pretty edgy – and you slam them with this thing, whatever it is she has . . .' Suddenly impatient, he rapped, 'Who am I trying to convince? It works, you see?'

I said, 'Get off my foot, monk,' and went on watching the screen. I don't think anyone else noticed the utility man. I hardly did myself.

'Hey,' Donato said suddenly, 'our generators are out, right? How do we get out of here?'

'When the bomb blows – no more D-field. Simple.'

England barked, just as suddenly, 'And what of all those missiles with the damper gone? They shoot off in every –'

'Dry up, clown,' said the skipper. 'And keep your panic to yourself. Every one of those missiles is triggered from one place and one place only – that planetoid. How do you think they were kept inside the Barrier and off the Luanae worlds all this time? Who cares if they get their power and explosives again? There'll be nobody in the driver's seat any more. Now shut up. She ought to blow pretty quick.'

'Blow how? If it's right in the middle of the – uh – damping field –'

'I said shut up! That isn't a cold-fusion bomb, it's a hairy old thermonuclear that doesn't give a damn what anybody believes.'

'What is it? What's going to happen? What's out there? Where –' (in rising panic).

'Go on back to bed, monk,' I said out of the side of my mouth, watching the screen. I meant it to sound kind – he'd had a bad time, but it didn't come out kind. I guess I'll never get used to talking to them.

It let go.

Oh, my God.

Captain Steev was wrong. There was triggering, somewhere, in some part of that split second of hell. Because all the missiles went too. They didn't fly, they didn't hunt. The warheads went.

It took a long time for our eyes to come back. The peeper screen was gone for good.

The turbine moaned down and down the scale and stopped. The lights stopped that annoying side-of-the-eye flicker.

'We got to go out and get Virginia,' was the first complete sentence anyone said.

Somebody laughed. Not a funny laugh.

England's voice was harsh. 'Don't be stupider'n you have to be, monkey. Don't you see we're back on our cold-fusion plant?'

'That makes no difference to him,' I told England. 'He wasn't around when the skipper explained.'

'Who wasn't around?' barked the skipper. 'Damn it,

139

Blum, nobody told you to leave your quarters. You're confined, you understand that? You, Palmer, can't I trust you to —'

'Wait!' The scream was almost more than a man could take. It was almost like that flare of light. The monkey stood there in the middle of the messhall, going mad again. 'Wait, wait, *wait!* I got to know. You all know, I don't. What *happened*?'

'Come on, Blum,' I said quickly. I was afraid of him but I think I was more afraid of the skipper. He had a look on his face I never want to see any more.

He brought the face close to Blum and said, 'You want to know, well okay, and I don't see why I should waste time or pity on a goddam monkey. That bomb knocked off the planetoid and the Barrier, which is what we came here for, and it knocked off your Virginia because that's what she was sent out for. Okay?'

'What you want to kill her for?' Blum whispered.

'You wouldn't happen to know any other way to bring back our power plant, now would you?' snarled the skipper.

I tried to explain to him. 'She didn't believe the plant could work, Blum. So it couldn't work.'

'I could make her believe. I could. I could.'

We looked at him, the big tilted head, the trembling nostrils. He wasn't going to get crazy mad after all. He was going into something else. It scared me. I don't mind saying.

He said, 'It was you, wasn't it, fixed it so she wouldn't believe anything.'

'She had a head start,' said the skipper, and turned his back. 'Come on, Potter. Donato. You're crew now, like it or not. Let's get this can the hell home. We got news for the people.'

'I never thought people could be like that,' Blum said very quietly. 'I never believed they could.'

'Get to bed, monk,' I said. And before I could stop

140

myself I begged him. 'Please,' I said, 'please, Blum – get out of his way.'

He looked up into my face for a long time. Suddenly he said, 'All right, Palmer.' Then he just went away.

I felt a lot better. Does you good to know you can handle men.

'Bunk in, men. We jump in five minutes.' He went forward to check his controls.

'Well, don't stand there,' I barked at them. 'Bunk in, men.'

'You know what, Palmer, you're a jerk,' Donato told me. Then we all bunked down.

Four minutes went by. Five. I heard the whir of machinery.

The lights went out. The whir was a moan, then a whine. The light came on dim, then bright, and flickering at the edges of the eyes.

I didn't figure it for any of my business, so I just lay there and waited. Pretty soon the skipper came back. He leaned against my cabin door and looked at me.

'Something the matter?' I wanted to know, trying to sound intelligent.

'Power plant's out, is all.'

'Oh,' I said. 'Uh – what's wrong with it?'

He heaved a slow sigh. 'Nothing. I checked it. Only it doesn't work.'

'I guess I better get up,' I said.

'Why?' he asked me, and went away.

I got up anyway and went and told Donato and Potter and England. They stayed where they were. They didn't like this quiet skipper with the quiet voice and no arguments. 'You know, if he can't fix it, we don't go anywhere. The Luanae have no ships, and we can't reach any of their planets,' England told me. I'd as soon he hadn't. I went to see Blum, for something to do.

He had his eyes open without seeing anything, and he was mumbling to himself. I tried to hear.

'. . . a little kid, they say you have the same chance as everybody else, you believe them, I'll hold your bag, they say, while you get the tickets, don't worry I'll be here when you get back, and you believe them. . . . Got a great job for you son, light work, big tips –'

'Monkey,' I said.

He looked up at me. 'You know what, Palmer, she said if you don't believe anything at all, you lose nothing when it all comes straight at last. It's all come straight for me now, Virginia. I can be safe now, Virginia, not believing; they can't take anything away from you that way, you're so right.'

He went on talking like that for a long time. I left and walked forward and found the skipper. He was in the control room jiggling a handle back and forth and not looking at it.

I said, 'Cap'n, that D-field the girl had – now, could a person fall into that by himself, I mean, without those Earth Planet doctors and all?'

'You sure you have to come bother me about it?' he said in a whisper, not looking at me. I backed way off and said, 'I think I do. I think the monkey's got a case of the same.'

'Now that's crazy! He'd have to have a real shock to get into a state like that. The monkey's okay. Beat it.'

'He's mumbling how he don't believe in anything.'

So the skipper went aft with me. He watched the utility monkey for a time and then said, 'Well, we'll fix it so he don't believe one way or another,' and hit the man in the bed on the jaw so he slid up and banged his head on the inboard bulkhead.

I could hear him breathing and I could hear the steam turbine, on and on. I said, 'I guess being unconscious doesn't make any difference to what you believe.'

'You should know,' said the captain. 'All right, Palmer, pick him up and bring him along.'

'Where?'

'Shut up.' He walked out. I guessed I'd better go along with him. I heaved and grunted the monkey up over my shoulder. I almost fell down with him. The captain was waiting in the corridor. He started to walk when I came out, so I followed him. We went down to pod level and forward to the airlock. Captain Steev began to undog the inner lock.

'What you going to do?' I asked him.

'Shut up,' said the captain.

'You fixing to kill this monkey?'

'You want to get home?'

'I don't know,' I said. I thought about it. The captain flung back the inner door and stood up. He said, 'What's your trouble, Palmer?'

I said, 'I don't think I'm going to let you do this, captain. There's some other way. You don't have to kill no little utility man.'

'Put him in, Palmer.'

I stood there with the limp monkey on my shoulder and glared at him while he glared back. I don't know how that might have ended (I do, but I'm ashamed to say it), but there was a noise and a voice, and somebody stood up out of the lock.

'Well it's about time,' Virginia said. 'You had the inner lock dogged and I've been lying in there for an hour. I guess I went to sleep. Who's that? What's the matter with Nils?'

The skipper looked like a man with a cup of flour in the face. '*Who told you to leave the pod?*'

'The Luanae,' she said calmly. 'Inside my head, like. It was funny. Told me how to get into the flight suit and how to get the gas bottles and strap them all together and use them to jet clear of the pod and that big gold thing. I got a long way away and then they told me to get back of a big piece of rock floating there. There was a lot of light . . . they told me when to go again, after the pieces stopped flying by. It was easier then. There's a jet

143

unit built right into the suit, did you know that? The Luanae told me how to use it.'

I got my jaw working and said, 'What made you think you could make it go?'

'Well, it's the same kind of unit that brought us here, isn't it? You have to believe your own eyes.'

At last the captain moved. Before he could say a word I slung the monkey down to the deck and pushed him. I bet the captain has been hit in his life, and maybe kicked, and all that, but I don't believe anyone just up and pushed him in the chest. He sat right down like a child with his legs spraddled out, looking up at me. 'Now you just stay there and shut up yourself,' I told him. 'You're always doing everything with these people the wrong way.'

Virginia was kneeling beside the monkey. 'What is it? What happened to him?'

I said, 'He got a bump, that's all. Listen, if you don't mind me asking, do you believe he loves you?'

'Oh yes,' she said immediately.

'Then I tell you what. You stay right here with him and rock him back and forth a little till his eyes open, hear? Then tell him that; tell him you believe him. That's all.'

The captain scrambled to his feet and opened his mouth to bellow. I bellowed first. I don't know where it came from, but I believed I could do it, and it was a time to believe things. 'You! You get up forward and check your controls. This can's going to take off like a scalded eel if you've left the controls open, and I don't want these folks shaken up. Go on, quick! You're the only one here knows how to do that. I'm the only one knows how to do this other. Right? Right!' I said and pushed him. He growled at me but he went right up the ladder.

I hunkered down beside those two people and looked them over. I felt fine, very fine. I said, 'Virginia, you
144

know what this is? This is the day everything all comes out straight. Right? Right.'

'You're a funny sort of man, Mr. Palmer.'

'A clown, ma'am.' I made a face at her and went up the ladder. About the time I reached the top the ship began to move. I fell right back down again, but they didn't think it was funny. They didn't even seem to see me. I climbed back up quietly and went back to my cabin.

HOW TO KILL AUNTY

'Little devil,' said the old lady admiringly, which was odd, because she detested squirrels, especially when they were after the birdseed and suet set out on the feeder. Birds make a great deal of difference to the bedridden. Yet, 'Oh, but you *have* got a brain in your head,' she murmured, for the squirrel, after two futile attempts to climb out to the feeder, was making for the slender branches directly above it.

Squirrels she detested, and unpunctuality, physical sloppiness, rice pudding, greed, advertising (especially TV commercials, of which she saw a great many), dull-wittedness and Hubert. Hubert, her nephew, was not a dish of rice pudding nor a squirrel, but he embodied everything else on the list.

Partly.

Maybe that was it, she thought, admiring the detestable squirrel. Right down the line, from how Hubert looked to what he did (he was an assistant producer — that is, general factotum, bottlewasher, squeezer of shaving cream on to whipped-cream desserts, source of yes-sirs for all the business and all the talent — for a TV commercial packager) Hubert was what she detested — partly. Even mostly. But in no case altogether.

That squirrel now, she thought, leaning out, reaching up over the bed for the brass handle which swung there; that squirrel is *all* squirrel, the pretty little, speedy little criminal. Letting her weight come on the handle, she reached for the loop of quarter-inch rope which hung from a brass fairlead sunk into the window frame. Holding it carefully, she worked her way back to the centre of the bed, let go the brass handle, and sat alertly watching the scene outside. At the very instant the admirable, damnable squirrel dropped from the tree-branches toward the feeding deck, the old lady pulled on the cord, and the feeder, sliding up its guy wires, moved out from under the animal, which snatched vainly at it, then hurtled down spraddle-legged to the lawn. It bounced like a rubber toy, then scampered angrily away, its tail drawing exact trajectories of each long bound.

A little out of breath, the old lady swore cheerfully at it and released the rope, so that the feeder slid back to its resting place among the outer shoots of the birch tree. Like certain other devices around the place, the feeder was her deft idea and Hubert's ham-handed workmanship. There again, she reflected. He wasn't altogether three-thumbed. He *could* turn out a job of work. But he got things right only by trying every wrong way first. She shuddered at the memory of the weeks of bully-ragging she'd put him through to get it done. Anyway, it worked, and could be drawn up to her window every morning to be filled.

She glanced at the clock and put her hand under her pillow for the remote control switch of the television. She saw a lot of television, and, unabashedly, she enjoyed it. Especially now. She enjoyed this particular television set even when it wasn't turned on. Hubert was trying to kill her with this television set, and she was knocking herself out trying to help him.

This was a totally different project from any bird-feeder. That had been done by nag and prod. The TV operation was far more subtle; suggestion, planned convenience, and an imitated stupidity on her part which Hubert was too stupid to know was imitated. And yet – she'd reluctantly admit – there was a certain doggedness about Hubert, this time. Of all the 'almost' things he was, about this one thing he really seemed willing to plug along until he got what he wanted.

He had first tried to kill her – oh, a long time ago,

now. It was because of Susie Karina. Well, perhaps there were other things, going back years, but Susie brought it to a head. Susie was a housemaid, and like a fool the old lady had let her live in, never dreaming that Hubert would make a fool of himself over any woman, but if he did, it wouldn't be Susie. Well, she'd been wrong about that. The old lady was never wrong about money or pulleys or birds or bonds or timing gears, but in the course of her long and lively life, so filled with things to do to keep herself to herself – every dime she had, she had earned – she had bypassed the intricacies of this Thing that seems to be going on between men and women all the time. It was the one area where she could guess wrong, and she certainly did this time. Susie was a small, downcast, black-banged little thing with bite-able lips and a heart full of greed. The old lady was not quite as wrong about Hubert – ordinarily he wouldn't have dared to raise his hat to a doxie on a desert island, so certain was he of his unfailing un-attractiveness to women – but neither he nor his aunt reckoned on Susie's barbarous ability to slide out of the camouflage and light fires with damp fuel. Score a man for his technique with women and you've drawn the height of his defences, give or take a little; so a man like Hubert, whose total experience had been a game of post office when he was ten (by unanimous vote the girls sent him to the dead-letter room) was about as hard to get to as the bottom of a ski slope from halfway down.

It had actually gone on for months, right in her house, right under her nose. Not only was the girl quiet and, at her specialty, clever, not only was the old lady tuned to other wave lengths; Hubert was so benumbed by the experience that even this intimate aunt could not tell his change from the norm. He did not begin to stay out nights, not sit and moon any more than his usual great deal, and there were no financial flurries at all – Susie coldly set her sights higher than her hat, even a new one.

148

The old lady, of course, did not know this, even after the silent discovery and quiet excision of the menace. It was quite by accident that she glanced down the stairwell at half-past two one morning and saw her nephew emerging from, of all places, the dining-room, of all things blowing kisses into it. The old lady slipped back into the shadows and had ample opportunity to watch Hubert ascend, grinning fatuously and carrying not only his shoes but his underwear. He passed the thunderstruck watcher all unknowing and entered his room and shut the door, whereupon his aunt, a spry old girl and very fast on her feet, dusted down the stairs like a windblown oatstraw and appeared in the dining-room door.

Four wide solid ancient chairs were placed side by side on the heavy rug, and at the rear end of the row hung a dark blouse and a white brassiere. At the far end, for one brief second full of shock and scorching hate, stood Susie Karina, clad in the skirt which matched the blouse. The faint glow from the tiny night light in the hall was enough to photograph the scene for both of them forever; then Susie melted backwards into the black shadows and disappeared. Without hesitation the aunt followed — it was the butler's pantry — and shot the heavy bolt on the dining-room side. She then stepped round to the kitchen and locked the other pantry door. Not a word was spoken; save for the snicking of the bolts, there was no sound.

The aunt made the rounds downstairs, being sure that everything was locked up tight — except for the pantry window, which opened easily into the wide wide world — and then, taking the garments from the dining-room between thumb and forefinger and holding them not quite at arm's length, she took them to the maid's quarters where she briskly and neatly packed all of the girl's possessions. She secured, from the wall safe, two weeks' wages, added that to the luggage, and strapped it

149

up. She took it to the kitchen, unlocked the back door, set the two suitcases upon and between the garbage cans, went inside, locked up and went to bed.

She did not know women, but she did know Hubert, and she knew Susie knew Hubert, and that Hubert's reaction to any scene, any emergency, would be blindly to do as he was told, and not by Susie. How long it took Susie to ponder this out she was never to know, but that Susie got the message was clear the next morning when the aunt looked out and saw the luggage gone.

Hubert still healthily slept. The aunt prepared breakfast and then called him commandingly. When, yawning and yapping, he entered the dining-room, she said, 'Put the chairs back, Hubert.' Hubert looked once into the kitchen, once at the spectacle of his aunt carrying a tray, and then the blood drained from his face. He put the chairs back. He sat on one. He ate his breakfast.

Actually the only thing that was ever said directly about the episode was said two nights later, when, after dinner, he rose casually and sauntered, with all the skilled histrionics of a spear-bearer on the first night of a high-school play, out to the hall tree where his hat hung. His aunt then spoke: 'A private detective will follow you wherever you go. He reports to Mr. Silverstein.' Now it happened that Mr. Silverstein, who was the lawyer who changed bequests in wills and all that, was also the silent and controlling partner in the advertising agency in which Hubert had just then begun.

Hubert paused. His wage was small and his address excellent. His expenses were almost nothing and his comfort considerable. His ability to provide these things – or anything at all – for himself was negligible. He left his hat where it was and went upstairs without a word. In due course they retired for the night.

Now it must be said that up to this point the old lady's actions had most genuinely been motivated by concern for Hubert; he could certainly not pursue his career properly in a town this size in such company as Susie Karina, even if the arrangement were legitimized; he had too much going against him as it was. And she had no intention, then, of punishing him. In her odd way, she felt the stirrings of respect for him — not for his specific acts, the charm of which was lost on her, but for his extraordinary success in pulling wool over her sharp old eyes. For she was, to the bone, an admirer of virtuosity, for its own sweet sake. She admired the music, for example, of Fritz Kreisler, not for its music, but for its fingermanship. She admired the better circus jugglers for the same reason and to the same degree. She owned a piece of jade carved with some symbols which, had she tracked them down, would have led her to a truly remarkable history, but her only interest in it was that it consisted of eight filigree balls, one inside the other, all freed from the same stone; never mind what it represented, where it had been, by whom owned to whom it meant what; just look at that for a clever thing, now! So for this gleam of deftness in her lump of a nephew she was happy to forgive and forget — though she saw no reason to reward him for it. Or to replace what it had cost him.

Mrs. Carstairs, the new maid, certainly did not. She immediately took over Susie's place, space and responsibilities — a weary soul who wore an aura of such a nature that the less the distance from her, by the inverse square law, the more one felt one had been munching saltpetre. Mrs. Carstairs was there asleep — actually, it was only her second night in the house, when it happened.

Again it was in the earliest hours of the morning, and again the big house was illuminated only by the speck of light glowing in the imitation brazier in the hall.

The aunt woke in that sudden, silent fashion which marks alertness to a sound which had now ceased; an opening of the eyelids with a click, a throat-throbbing,

151

instant eagerness to pursue the very last echo of something gone but vitally important. The old lady threw off the covers and rolled to a sitting position and, in spite of the hard difficult thump of her heart, held her breath.

She heard a low, happy, whispering laugh. She barely heard it. It was unvoiced, and came from somewhere indeterminate.

She rose to her feet, and again held her breath.

She heard the childish, effortful sound of someone emphasizing a kiss: mmmm — *yuh!*

She ran on tiptoe to her door, across from which was the head of the stairs, and stopped again to listen.

What moved her, what sent her moving, sprinting, springing to the stairs was nothing at all. But *nothing*, not a sound, not a breath. She could have borne anything else, but not this waiting for the next sigh, smack, chuckling tongue-cluck; not this wondering *where*, wondering who. . . . How? Mrs. Carstairs, did she know every lock, did . . . or was it — and so she sprang.

And her first foot, the right foot, to step off the landing, flew out and up, dragging the other with it, and so she lay in the air. After that the observations, the memories they painted, were not so sharp. She was sure something dark and rectangular flew away, out and down, as she lay in the air, and curved to the steps below: the cruel crash at the base of her spine and the small of her back (but no no no pain, horribly no pain!) and her elbows; and oh, that was the agony.

It was dark already; it did not grow dark for her; the dark grew black. But in the last clouded second before eclipse, she seemed to see a small someone dart from the dining-room, scoop up the rectangular thing, a thing thicker than a briefcase, not as wide or long, and flick away with it. Then a flash of light as Mrs. Carstairs came fumbling into the hall — only a flash because of the greater flash of torture from her elbows, and the black.

Eleven years.

Eleven years she thought about it. You can think a lot in eleven years. You can think a lot in bed. You can think a whole lot in eleven bedridden years.

It doesn't have to drive you crazy, knowing you'll never walk again, not even when you had always walked, yes, run, yes, up until so recently skiied, skated, trudged, hiked. (Never danced, though: now, now that was a good thing.)

What happened that night? Was it what she remembered? She could never quite be sure. And what had happened that she did not see or know about? She'd never know. No one, after Mrs. Carstairs and Hubert came tumbling sleepily out (they always claimed they heard nothing but the fall) and the doctors and ambulance and police were in and out, nobody could possibly piece together which doors were locked, or whether the pantry window had been closed. What she said about dark rectangles flying under her feet, about kissings and laughter somewhere – they listened so carefully to the way she talked that they frightened her, and she mentioned them no more. She might have, ten years later when Mrs. Carstairs, grown slow and hobbly, was cleaning out the pantry and found the old-fashioned carpet sweeper thrown far under the big solid maple butcher table. It had no stick and the brushes were worn away, but it had four good wheels and it was just exactly large enough to hide in the shadows, say, on one step of a flight of stairs. But the aunt never saw it, and Mrs. Carstairs never mentioned it; why should she? It wasn't good for anything, and besides, it had a big dent in the top as if it had been stepped on; so she just threw it away; it lay for a day on the garbage cans, looking like a little suitcase.

There was Susie Karina; what ever happened to Susie Karina? Why, she got a better deal from another nothing, name of Smith or something, whose important father owned a car dealership dealing in cars so important they sold themselves; the younger Smith was called the salesman. She married him, and he really loved her, which she didn't fully realize until he shot her as she was about to make a still better deal for herself. So she no longer mattered to Hubert and his aunt if, indeed, she ever really had. The big thing in their lives was each, the other; Susie had just cleaned up the issue.

Bedridden, the aunt now imprisoned him. He had tried to kill her (or the girl had, which was altogether the same thing) and for that she flung her coils around him, coils of business, of banking, of guilt and habit and demand (the threat kind of demand: the sheer nuisance kind of demand). Numb, bound, inarticulate, helpless, he stayed. The only wrinkle in the gelid stream of his life was when he had left the low level of the advertising business which would have lasted the rest of his life had he stayed, for a lower level in television; and anyone but Hubert could see that in some years' time he would elevate himself to about where he had been in advertising, and stay *there* for the rest of his life.

And what did Hubert think about? It is quite possible he thought not at all; this he was equipped for. But he could feel, and his aunt saw to it that he did. She wasped and prodded him and sat him down and walked him away; she would demand his presence and then not talk to him, but stare into the flat bland silver eye of the television to which she was addicted, and if he shifted his feet she would shush him. And she read aloud to him — car repair manuals, and highly specialized articles on bird food, and legal reviews and murder stories, during all of which he sat mute and moist outside — he was one of those heavy-set men with a shiny face — but puckering a bit from some internal drying. Or she would talk to him: 'My, Hubert, how little it takes to kill a man, how much sometimes! Why, remember Doc Maginn, so hale and happy, stepped on a needle in the pile of his

154

bedside rug, dead in a week. Yet I've seen basket cases from the First War, Hubert, everything shot away, legs, arms, eyes, voice, hearing; still they live. You can live a long time in a basket, Hubert, in a bed. Keep yourself alert, keep busy doing something, keep your mind alive; have someone to wait on you — why — you can last forever that way, Hubert. Hubert, get up. Sit over there.' And Hubert would get up and sit down again over there, moved because she felt like moving him. Oh, she hated him. Oh, she was going to kill him, she was killing him; and the weapon she chose was time and abrasion; she was going to outlast him, she was going to hammer out the length of her life thin and sharp and long, long, and ease it into him up to the hilt till he was dead of it. 'Now put me to bed, Hubert, put your old aunty to bed. Close the blinds. Open the window. Hubert,' she would snap if he began to decelerate, '*pay the rent!*' He paid nothing in cash; he never had; he knew what she meant. Earn your keep, do as you're told, be what you're for: *pay the rent*. So every night he turned the TV to face her bed, he lowered the blinds, opened the drapes, opened or shut the window, checked the heat.

She knew how everything worked; he understood none of it. By how many leaves of the old-fashioned one-pipe steam radiator were hot, she could tell him where to set the thermostat downstairs. By the size of the picture on her TV she could tell how much voltage drop occurred in the line, and by the way it changed, she could tell what caused it, and she knew the difference between the effect of Mrs. Carstairs' ironing downstairs, and the use of the rotisserie in their neighbours' house. She could splice rope, and taught Hubert by the hour because he could not learn: 'Worm and parcel with the lay, turn and serve the other way,' she'd chant at him, and watch him do it wrong even while he repeated it. She invented things and made him build them. She had him fix a brass handle to a rope from the beam overhead, so she could reach the window sill or turn the TV to face the bed when he wasn't there, or, after the weeks it took him to rig it, the bird-feeder. And a headboard with shelves and a buzzer and light to call him when he was asleep and one to call Mrs. Carstairs. And a sick-room tray with a little vice and a rack for hand tools. And inventions on the inventions. A plaited rawhide grip for the brass handle. A floor stand for the workbench so it didn't bounce when she used the jack-plane. Remote controls for the TV: on, off, volume, phone jack, in the days before they sold them with sets. She had lived a variegated and busy life, in the long process of doing something instead of the something she did not understand. She was a pioneer of all the Rosie-the-Riveters, going to work in a Liberty engine plant as a young girl; she was tiny then, and the only one in the place with hands small enough to adjust the carburettor heat controls from inside. She had been the first woman to be called Yachtsman at the Bar Harbour Club, recklessly slamming a Star-class forerunner in the regatta. She was a court reporter and studied law and was a legal secretary – actually running a firm for the figureheads. She made a lot of money and invested skilfully and made more, and hung on to every dime of it. Now she had all this to devote to Hubert. Life was full. Life always had been full.

Then Hubert tried to kill her again. She saw it coming right from the very first, and just watched it come, wondering what on earth he was up to. He was sneaking into her room when she was in the bathroom, doing something, sneaking out. She soon found out what it was. He was loosening the screws in the back of the TV.

It took days. He seemed to be operating on four across the top, three down the side. She said nothing to him about it. He did nothing else differently. He sat and was read to and cut his thumb on a spokeshave, making

156

her laugh, and later, when she came out of the bathroom on her wheelchair — it was more table than chair, for it hurt her to sit up, and she hated it — she would stop and check, and sure enough, he'd slipped in and loosened them a bit more.

She could have stopped him in a second, with a word, but she was fascinated. It went on for five days; on the morning of the sixth, after he had gone to work, she got settled for her morning of TV and found the set wouldn't work. With her ring-on-a-rope holding her up, she reached for the set and swivelled it around on its lazy-suzan base. She pulled out three of the loose screws and was able to bend the hardboard back plate far enough to peer inside.

Tubes were gone.

She lay and pondered that. Was he (tender gesture) trying masterfully to help her cut down on her excessive viewing? Or was this just a childish and spiteful annoyance? Surely even Hubert knew better than that! Why, for that he'd pay . . . oh Lord, for years he'd pay!

No, it was more than that. He was doing something in his bumbling way. Only there had to be more to it.

'Hubert,' she said that evening after she had summoned him (she would not permit him to eat with her), 'something's wrong with the TV.'

He did not act surprised or try any play-acting, beyond saying with a rehearsed kind of promptness, 'All right I'll take it down to be fixed tomorrow,' all in a flat uninflected voice; then he sat down where she told him to. She talked to him and read to him; but there was a welcome difference in the air; why, almost half the time she actually realized he was there.

In the morning he grunted and bumped it downstairs, and in the afternoon came bumping and grunting, a coloured man helping him, with a new set. A new grey modern streamlined set with a bigger screen than the old one, and a smaller case rather unaccountably designed to offer the least possible resistance to wind. 'What on earth is that?'

'The other one is shot,' Hubert informed her. 'The man said so. I bought this one.'

'It's horrible.'

'I already bought it,' said Hubert with a kind of faint doggedness.

She snorted and told him how to attach two wires to the back and how to stick the plug in the socket. It had a very nice remote control on it, with a station selector as well as volume, and on-off. She was mollified as far as the set was concerned; but what on earth was his play?

She found out the next afternoon when Mrs. Carstairs hobbled up with her arthritis and the mail. Alone with it, she found tucked among the ads and the bills and the magazines, a periodical which she knew, the instant she saw it, was late, though she had not missed it until now. It was a consumer's magazine – one of those outfits which tests goods bought on the open market. The old lady always read the very print off it; she spent her money, she used to say, she didn't throw it away.

Why late? And why had the little semicircular seal that kept it closed in the mail been slit?

Hubert? Had he picked it up, kept it a while, then dropped it in the mailbox on his way to work? *Why?*

She riffled the pages. Soaps, hand-held can openers, table-model TV's, an Italian vs a French miniature car.... *Table-model TV!* Oh, that was all. He just wanted to be sure and get one that was recommended.

She looked at the listing. It was there, all right. There was even a picture of it. As to the recommendation – it was heartily, earnestly, explicitly *not*. For this was the make and model, even (she checked this laboriously, swinging perilously at the edge of the bed by her strong right hand holding the ring from the ceiling) within a dozen digits of the serial number – the very same lethal contraption which, ungrounded and suffering slight damage from the overtightening of one hold-down screw between chassis and the metal case, had already killed a man and a boy.

She looked at the picture and the diagrams, and then at the set: 'Oh!' she cried in sheerest delight, throwing the magazine high in the air, 'How *cute!*'

Poor precious Hubert, nursing the place inside him where most people keep the embers of hate, but which, in him, must certainly be a clean little barely warm pot of pasteurized mush; oh, how cute! numbly associating her with TV, TV with her, until one day – when was it? four, five months ago, he heard about this set in the news; oh how he must have mumbled and gnashed on the idea; how long must it have taken him to find one? How hard did he have to think before he plotted out the fiendishly clever idea of getting tubes out of her old set and claiming it was finished? Oh, she thought, the little darling. He's really trying.

That night, for the first time in years, his numbed shiny face seemed to move a little from inside, as if some good fluid were soaking the parched places under the moist skin; for she was kind to him. She was unquestionably laughing at him, but she was kind to him.

The next day, after Mrs. Carstairs had cleaned up, Hubert's aunt fumbled through her workbench and tools, and found a lamp socket and some heavy wire. She connected two foot-long leads and screwed in a bulb after testing it. She chuckled the whole time, even when she underwent the pain of bringing her wheelchair alongside and agonizingly rolling into it. Grunting with pain and chuckling with laughter, she got to the corner and put one wire against the steam pipe and the other against the metal side of the new set.

Nothing.

Using the remote control, she clicked the set on. Again she touched one wire to the set, the other to the pipe.

Still the bulb did not light. There was nothing wrong with this set.

Hubert . . . poor, poor old Hubert.

For a limp moment she ignored the pain and lay in the chair, wagging her head from side to side in wordless pity.

This was as far as the poor addlehead could think. Get a set like the one that had killed some people. Get it next to her. . . . What passed next in his fogbound mind could only have been, '. . . and then maybe some way she . . .'

She could shake him, the poor darling! Didn't he know that to be electrocuted by house current, the electricity had to flow through the body? Stand in a puddle, preferably with a good iron drain in it, and stick your hand in a fuse box; then maybe. Or hold a water pipe and put a wet thumb in a socket — then perhaps. But he must, with millions of other people, share the notion that you could be killed by, for example, current running from one side of your fingertip to the other side of the same finger . . . or maybe the poor thing just didn't have a notion at all.

Back in bed at last, and rested, she began to think of Hubert with pity and tenderness. He'd worked *so* hard . . . and she wasn't thinking of lugging TV sets up and down stairs, either.

And such a clever idea, too, in its way. If he only knew what he was doing.

She thought about it, and about him, all day long; and when at last she knew what she was going to do, it was as if all the clocks in the world had stopped; oh, how she ached for him to be here; oh, how she wanted him near! Suddenly the world was bright again for her who had not realized how dark it had become; here out of the gloom had come the loveliest . . . oh, the most wonderful thing to plan, to work on.

Hubert needed help.

He couldn't possibly do this by himself. He had to learn, to plan, to fix, to arrange. And above all he had to feel he was doing it by himself, because he wanted it so; anyone who worked so hard had to want it very much. But it would be no good unless he was sure, all along the line, that it in all its parts was his own doing.

So when he came upstairs that evening, and when she had portrayed enough surliness with him to make him unsuspicious, she began.

'*Hubert!*' It was said with a slightly rising inflection; in the spectrum of her summonses, this one stood on the line that said 'Get to work'. He started uneasily.

'My ring,' she said, pointing to her leather-handled, rope-dangled helper. 'That rope stretches all the time.'

He looked at with dim eyes. 'Looks okay.'

'Well, you don't have to use it. I want you to put up something that won't stretch.'

He tried hard. She could see him at it, like a toothless man gumming a steak. 'Chain,' he said at last.

She argued with him scornfully. Chain was pinchy and noisy. Wire rope would fray after a time, sharp and splintery. And at last she had led him to braided copper cable, which would be handsome, and though it would stretch, it would stretch just so much and no more; and then she led him like Socrates, asking, demanding and argumentative question after question, until he had no choice but to devise a big wide ring in the beam above, a second ring in the beam in the corner, and anchorage to something solid there, thus the cable could be taken up as it stretched, until it would stretch no more. Laboriously he wrote down his shopping list, and she spent a delicious night and day anticipating, and two more happy evenings hammering at him until he had it just right. And all the while she savoured the delightful, and quite correct, thought that he still did not realize how very beautifully that new cable would fit into 'his' sweet little plan. Oh, how she anticipated the moment of revelation! How proud he would be, and hopeful. This, she thought, is living. Where's the woman, she thought (she often compared herself with, categorically, 'women') who with all her so-called wiles, who knows what this is like, to lead a poor dear man step by step — no; inch by inch — down the very path you planned for him, and all the while let him think he's the one, he's the one?

She had not felt like this in years. She had never felt like this. She *liked* it. She liked it so much she let the whole thing rest for two days, while happily she planned the next step the all-powerful male must take.

'Oh ... *Hub*ert!' This in descending tones; this was the disappointment, the 'how *could* you!' salutation.

'Whuh? Whuh?' he said rapidly, worriedly.

She held up the consumers' magazine. 'Of all the TV sets in the whole wide world, why did you buy this one?'

He wet his lips. 'Seems pretty okay.'

'Here!' she snapped. (Not even 'come here'.) He rolled to his feet and came, peering at the magazine. She demanded, 'What are you trying to do — kill me?'

He opened his mouth, closed it, lifted his hands and let them fall. Finally he said, 'Well, I got it awful cheap.'

Aloud, she read the account of the deaths. 'I don't doubt you got it cheap,' she snorted, then looked up. 'How cheap?'

He said, 'A hundred and twenty off list.'

'Oh, well,' she said; and inside she hugged herself: oh, what fun!

She changed the subject. She said the rawhide on the brass handle hurt her hand, and she made him find her utility knife and cut it away. While he nicked and picked at it, she read aloud the other part of the article, where it said that the set was otherwise very fine. She sounded almost as if she forgave him. Anyway she let up on him, and with her remote unit, turned the set on and they watched a crime show. Or he did. She watched him. At the part in the TV play where the murderer accomplished his evil deed – and it happened to be an old woman – she could have sworn his dull eyes acquired a dim shine. He even stopped picking away at the rawhide and sat down to watch absorbedly. For once she let him, and it was all right; of his own accord he went back to it after the show and finished the job. Oh you sweet boy, she thought, almost fondly, for once in your sloppy life you're *altogether* something; why you dear, you're just full of this thing.

She turned off the sound – but left the set on – with her control, thereby wrenching him out of the Western which succeeded the murder play. Perforce, he gaped at her. 'You *could* have killed me,' she said accusingly.

'There has to be something wrong with the set first,' he said doggedly. 'The set's all right, I tell you.'

'That may be,' she said. 'But look.' She reached for the brass handle above the bed and tugged at it. 'Look, I'm grounded.'

He shook his head, mystified.

'The radiator!' she yelped at him. 'Why did you have to anchor the cable to the radiator?'

He scanned the cable, up from her hand, across from one beam to the next, down to the radiator in the corner, behind the TV set. He shrugged, not understanding. 'You said anchor it to something solid.'

She had said to anchor it to the radiator, but she didn't give him a chance to remember that. 'Don't you see?' she shrilled. 'Suppose there was a short circuit to the TV case, the way it tells about in the magazine, and suppose I had to touch it, like turn it toward the bed. Don't you see I'd be holding a one with the other? Don't you understand *anything*?' She let him watch her cloudily, saw him swing his gaze from her to the cable, the TV set, back to her; saw the stirrings of that moment of revelation she had anticipated so much. 'Stupid, stupid, stupid!' she shrilled, '*this* is what I mean!' and she flung her weight on the handle and reached out for the TV set. 'See?' she said, slapping it. 'See?' she said, turning it on its swivel. She regained the bed.

How shiny his face was. Suddenly she wanted to mop up that dull excitement she could see moistening his parched core. She said coldly, 'Well anyway, I guess that proves the set's safe for now.'

Through her lashes she watched him. For a split second she thought he was going to cry. Then he slumped dejectedly and stared at the set. She knew what he was thinking as well as if his moist brow had been equipped with one of those electric signs with the moving letters. She knew he was thinking how close he had come, and how never in a thousand years would he be able to figure out the difference between this harmless object and the one he had hoped it would be. She imagined further thoughts – old familiar ones, doubtless, their path trodden smooth by his years of plodding hatred: So bash her head in (but Mrs. Carstairs, downstairs all the time . . .). Feed her a glass of warm milk with – (but he never brought her milk, and she certainly wouldn't touch it if he did).

. . . or maybe these were only her own imaginings; maybe he wasn't thinking at all. He could do that, she was sure. Ha! she'd soon enough turn them on again! She said, batting at the brass handle, and speaking very softly as if to herself, 'Couldn't get closer to certain death if you'd planned it,' and watching his widening eyes and the slight babyish protrusion of his lower lip, she just knew he was saying to himself, 'She knows. Oh my God, I bet she knows.'

She felt a thrill of anticipation. Get him scared; oh fine. Fear will make him move. And worry: let's make him worry a little. 'Tomorrow,' she said, 'we'll just have to put up something else besides that copper cable. Just *too* dangerous.' And she saw him look down into his hands and pout miserably. (Was he thinking, *I'll never get a chance like this again.* Sure he was.)

Oh, he looked so miserable! Oh, did any woman ever have such a toy as this? Let's bring back the hope now.

She swatted the magazine explosively, making him jump. 'It shouldn't be allowed!'

'Oh,' he mumbled, 'the factory called them all back in. All they could find.'

'I don't mean that,' she said, and hit the magazine again. 'This thing, with the photographs and diagrams and all. Why, you know what this amounts to, just this one picture of a screw tightened too much? Why, it's instructions, that's what it is; any fool could take a safe set and make a killer out of it, just by reading this. It shouldn't be allowed!' She took the magazine and flung it at his feet, making him jump again. 'Take the filthy thing out of here!'

His hands, she gloated, literally trembled as he picked it up. He rolled it and turned it over and over between his hands. It was like a caress. (Oh Hubert, she called silently, if you only knew how wonderful you are!) 'Yes, Aunty,' he said, his eyes on the magazine. He put it, rolled, into his back pocket, and rose.

'Put your old aunty to bed.'

'All right.' Preoccupied, he did all the things he had to do with the drapes, the shade, the heat, the TV, her covers, the lights. She was glad when he turned out the lights; it had been hurting her face not to smile openly.

What would he be thinking now? She knew: oh, she knew, especially because – 'Hu*bert*!' – because, silhouetted in the door, he already had the magazine out of his pocket, though it was still rolled. Ah, he could barely wait! Imagine – Hubert eager, Hubert dedicated, Hubert excited . . . and Hubert certainly wondering how on earth he would get the chance to make that one little change, turn that one screw just far enough to break the insulating washer. 'Hu*bert*!'

'Yes, aunty.'

'In the morning ask Mrs. Carstairs to turn up the hot water heater right after breakfast. I'm going to have a good long hot soak. Just this once I'm going to soak for a whole hour.'

He thought he was answering but his voice was lost in a peculiar abrupt wheeze. Smiling in the darkness, she asked, 'What, Hubert?'

'All right, Aunty; I'll tell her.'

He went away.

She soaked for more than an hour. She drowsed, almost fell asleep in the tub. In the first place she had been awake almost all night, smiling most of the time, making little bets with herself. Even with a clear photograph and a concise explanation, would Hubert be able to find the right screw? Could there be any guarantee he'd turn it the right way? Would he wait so long for the coast to be clear that he wouldn't have time to do it at all? She had forgotten, at first, about Mrs. Carstairs and the Saturday cleaning, which she would certainly do while the old lady was in the tub. She could all but see poor Hubert in his room down the hall, an ear cocked to the arthritic housekeeper's puttering about in his aunt's room, his eyes glued to the page in the consumer's magazine, reading it over and over, moving his lips. A killer.

Hubert, Hubert. Dear Hubert. Maybe the silly old thing wouldn't even try to fix the set. Mrs. Carstairs left at last. There was long, long silence. She began to doze.

A sharp sound snapped her out of it and she literally clapped her soapy hand over her mouth to keep in the burst of shrill laughter that filled her mouth and throat. For dear dedicated worried fearful Hubert, with the bone head and the ham hands, Hubert had dropped his screwdriver. The picture of him, round-eyed and whey-faced, staring in terror at the closed bathroom door, was almost more than she could bear.

More silence, a bit more hot water and another doze. She came to herself with a start, and looked with amused horror at her wrinkled fingerpads; she was as waterlogged as Davy Jones' floor mop. She began the arduous process of draining, drying, dressing, and loading the useless parts of herself on to the agonizing wheelchair. She took as long as possible ... long enough. He was not in her room when she opened the door.

Back in bed, she composed herself for her Saturday televiewing, and with her hand on the control, remembered. Then: why not? and she laughed and clicked it on.

The sun was out. The birds were out. Hubert was out (she laughed) shopping for rope for her helper-handle, for no matter what, he had his orders. (Oh the fool; what on earth does he think he could do with himself without *me*? But isn't he the one? Isn't he the gutsy boy, though?) The TV was excellent, all of it, even the commercials. She thoroughly enjoyed her afternoon.

At last he came up. She did not greet him; she wondered too much what he would say. She had been philosophizing about murder and the murderer: at what exact point did a man become a murderer? According to the law, when the victim died, be it a microsecond or forty years after the attack. But was that really so? When a man pulls a trigger, and the bullet is on its way, and it's too late for anything but death to happen, is he not already a murderer? Hubert now: Hubert had already pulled his trigger. She might have died any time today. As a matter of fact, she had lain impotently watching a big grey squirrel gobbling up all the suet from the feeder, because she had rather not take hold of that brass handle and swing herself so close to the TV in order to reach the feeder-rope.

And Hubert, out shopping: was he wondering if he

would come home to a curious sidewalk and the white wailing of ambulances? She had purposely not called him, and he had delayed downstairs until quite late, doubtless screwing up his courage for the trip upstairs to find – what? – in her room. Surely he had not reckoned on being the one to discover her. She could almost hear his half-articulate complaint: after all he had done, did he have to go through all that too?

She resisted a temptation to arrange herself sprawling on the carpet between the bed and the TV, to lie still until he bent over her, and then to start laughing; a sure instinct told her that this was the way, even with Hubert, to get herself not only murdered, but beaten to death along with it. She contented herself with lying as still and – what was the word? waxen was the word – as possible, with her eyes closed, until he stood over the bed and murmured, 'Aunty?'

She opened her eyes and he stepped back two paces and stood, not knowing what to do with his hands. Still she waited, to see what he would say next, and it was (the clumsy, blundering dunderhead), 'Watch some TV today, did you?'

She laughed and struggled up, elbow-walking back to her backrest. 'Lots, and it was fine. It's late.'

'Yes, I . . . think I'll go turn in.'

She tilted her head to one side and said, 'Had a tough day, Hubert?' and smiled at him. The quick, passing contraction of his features convinced her he was shouting silently to himself, 'She knows! She knows!'

'Well,' she said. 'You're going to put your old aunty to bed first.'

Did he hesitate? Did he really? Did he care? He seemed to be ready to turn and walk out . . . or did he turn to remind himself that downstairs the housekeeper kept a living ear, a remembering brain, and there must be no quarrel for her to remember? He said docilely, 'All right, aunty.'

'I think,' she said, 'I'll watch the late show tonight. I had a nap.'

'The late show, yes,' he echoed. He did the window blind and window things, the drape things. Passing the TV, which faced her, he hit it with his hip; it swung to face the door.

She nodded approvingly. She couldn't have done better herself. She said, 'Hubert – turn the TV to me.'

'All right,' he said. But instead he came over and straightened her covers. His face was especially shiny, and she could see the dark marking of damp where his hands touched the bed clothes.

She began to laugh.

For the first, and the last time in her life, she heard Hubert speak to her in the imperative: 'Don't laugh,' he said.

She subsided, but she took her time about it, laughing all the way. 'Funny boy.' Suddenly she cut it dead and said coldly, 'Turn that TV to me.'

His back was to the set: he stood between it and her. 'You can see it all right from there.' He held his right wrist hard with his left hand. She could see the shiver of the fabric of his trousers as his knees trembled.

'We don't want a quarrel for Mrs. Carstairs to hear,' she said carefully.

'Oh gosh no,' he said fervently.

A crazy situation. Extraordinary. Delightful. This, she thought, is living. 'Turn the set, Hubert.' She smiled. 'It won't bite you. It isn't even on.'

He wet his lips, so wet already. His hands were wet, his face and his mouth. His tears were wet, waiting to come. He whispered – she knew he didn't mean to whisper, but it was all he could manage – 'You can reach it.'

'All right,' she said suddenly, gently, with all the tones and overtones of complete capitulation.

'Well I.' He said it as if it were a complete and sensible statement, turned and marched to the door.

'*Hubert!*'

He stopped as if she had roped him. He was in the doorway; he stayed where he was and did not turn. He was like a machine with brakes locked and the clutch disengaged; but one could feel the motor racing; in the split tatter of a second it would be gone from there screaming.

'Please,' she said gently (to *Hubert*? Please?). 'You forgot to check the heat. You'll do that for me, won't you?'

His shoulders slumped and he turned back into the room. 'Oh, sure, I guess,' he said wearily. He crossed to the corner and leaned over and felt the radiator. It was the metal top of the TV set that he leaned over. His aunt moved her thumb *that* much on the remote control and turned the set on.

Hubert made the most horrible sound the aunt had ever heard; it was like a particularly raucous sneeze — *inward*. She had read that sometimes when a jolt first hits them they swallow their tongues, and then suffocate on them. That is what Hubert was doing. One stiff hooked arm rested on the top of the TV set, and the other stiff hooked arm rested on the radiator, and his legs stuck straight out behind him with the toes pointed, and quivered. Through the legs of his trousers, at the calves, could be seen muscle mounding up in cramps like golfballs.

'Kill *me*, will you?' croaked the aunt, but the set warmed up just then and roared and drowned her out. She turned the volume down and stared at Hubert's legs and pointing toes sticking out from behind the TV set, and knew with crushing certainty that from the very beginning she had set things up to come out this way. She didn't recall having purposely, consciously done so; she knew only that she must have, that's all. She glared at the legs and said, 'But you broke my back!'

All in all, that was a pretty good day. And night.

Living; really living. One of the best parts of all had to do with the police, who took all of fifteen seconds to sniff out that there was more to this 'accident' than met the eye. There was a young man with two deep measures of vivid intelligence for eyes, and a quick quiet voice; he asked almost exclusively important questions, one right after the other. Who brought that set in here? Who hung that cable from the radiator to a point over the bed? Well, if it was rope before, who substituted woven copper? Who took the leather grip off the brass handle?

Hubert, Hubert, Hubert.

Men came up and brushed fine white dust around the TV, and took off the back and brushed dust inside, and photographed everything. Whose fingerprints?

Finally, and funniest of all, was the man who regretted the accident, who assured her that the police expert had removed the short circuit, making the set now quite safe, but at the same time warning her to get rid of it, just in case. Lastly, he hemmed and he hawed and he suggested in extremely careful language that she should not attempt to bring an action against the set manufacturer in this particular case, in view of certain technicalities which we needn't go into at such a time as this 'but I faithfully assure you that if you don't take my advice you will only wish you had, and you will find out at great – ah – trouble to yourself that I was right.' In short, it was unanimously agreed to conceal from this little old bedridden lady that her nephew had got himself caught in the vicious trap he laid for her. Why bother her with it? The only thing that would ever force her to know it would be if she started lawsuits; lying there like a real little old protected female woman, waxen as possible, she agreed in a faint voice that they were right and she trusted them all. It was grand fun. Her finish didn't come until the next afternoon, when a sniffling Mrs. Carstairs brought her the things out of Hubert's room to sort. There wasn't much, and among the few papers was the copy of the consumers' magazine, still folded back open to the article about the metal-cased TV set. Over this Hubert had pondered and waited, and while waiting, had doodled, filling O's and putting moustaches on the faces of the consumers' electronicians in the photos. He had also written a sentence and a word.

It was as if Hubert had been denied understanding and intelligence and the ability to articulate, all his life, the formless clouds of feeling within him, in just and equal compensation for this single, simple, devastating insight. He had written:

Without me she is nothing but an old woman.

And under that, in very large, careful letters:

OLD

His aunt read this and closed her eyes to consider it, and that was the finish for her. When she opened her eyes again she looked at her hands, skinny and crooken-a-clawed, and she pulled at her sparse white hair, drawing it forward over her face to be able to look at it, through it. All her life she had been too busy to be loved, too busy to be liked. She had been too busy to have a childhood and she had been too busy to be old.

Not any more. The Hubert business was the last thing she had to be busy about; for years it had been everything and the only thing, and now she'd finished it, and though she lingered on for a long while, it was the finish for her.

CLOSE ENCOUNTERS OF THE THIRD KIND

Steven Spielberg

WATCH THE SKIES . . .

Close Encounter of the First Kind:
Sighting of an Unidentified Flying Object

Close Encounter of the Second Kind:
Physical evidence after UFO sighting

Close Encounter of the Third Kind:
Actual contact between human observers and
UFO occupants . . .

All over the world, millions of reliable witnesses,
including respected scientists, have been reporting
UFO sightings for the past thirty years. Experts
everywhere concede the overwhelming
probability of intelligent life elsewhere in the
Universe.

From these indisputable facts, Steven Spielberg,
brilliant young director of JAWS, has written a
frightening and significant book.

Now a major picture from Columbia Pictures

85p

0 7221 8081 0   FICTION/FILM TIE-IN

THE HUMANOIDS
Jack Williamson

'We serve and obey, and guard men from harm'

Those were the words that scientist Clay Forester had learned to dread. Those words were the code of the Humanoids – and the Humanoids had enslaved his world! Sleek, invincible, perfect machines, the Humanoids had been created to fulfil an ideal, but the ideal had got out of hand. Now they followed their Prime Directive with terrifying insistence. Men must be safe, so dangerous activities such as driving, flying – even walking unescorted – were forbidden. Men must be happy – so any dissatisfaction was removed with the aid of a hypodermic needle. Man was a helpless prisoner. Clay Forester could not rest until he had destroyed the robot invaders. But it seemed he was powerless to fight them – until a child with an incredible talent walked into his plans . . .

THE HUMANOIDS is a classic SF novel in the masterful tradition of Isaac Asimov's ROBOT series.

SCIENCE FICTION
0 7221 9176 6

LASER BEAMS FROM STAR CITIES?

Robin Collyns

MESSAGES FROM THE STARS . . . ?

Has the Earth been visited in previous ages by intelligent beings from outer space?

Are the visits still continuing?

Could laser beams be directed at our planet from space, as a form of attempted communication by another race?

Have they formed the strange cup-like impressions found on the surface of all the Earth's continents?

These are just some of the many fascinating and thought-provoking questions which Robin Collyns asks, and attempts to answer, in this original book. His research into extraterrestrial activity has thrown startling new light onto problems which have baffled man for far too long.

By the bestselling author of *Did Spacemen Colonise the Earth?*

0 7221 2457 0   75p